SECRETS IN SHADOWS

SIGNS OF LIFE SERIES
BOOK 6

CRESTON MAPES

ROOFTOP

PRAISE FOR *SECRETS IN SHADOWS*

"Creston's newest book was both a joy and a trap. I enjoyed reading, but my eyes didn't enjoy the strain . . . I simply couldn't stop reading until I reached the end!" — **Author (and fan girl) Sharon Srock**

"Mapes invites us back into the world of Veteran Portland Police Investigator Wayne Deetz with another fast-paced adventure filled with family drama, crooked cops and, as always, redemption. Another brilliant addition to the Signs of Life Series!" — **Watermark Christian Store - Director of Retail Operations Rachel Savage**

"The characters in the *Signs of Life* series have become my friends. I love the Deetz family! *Secrets in Shadows* delivers the suspense we have come to expect from Creston Mapes." — **Leader of the** *Finding Hope Through Fiction Book Club*, **Ginger Aster**

"Two words for *Secrets in Shadows*, the newest thriller from Creston Mapes: BUCKLE UP! This one will keep you turning pages at a breakneck speed. Set in the quagmire of Portland's gutted police force, thanks to corrupt politics at the highest levels, this one's got everything. Good cops/bad cops. The rippling effect of alcohol and drug abuse. Family relationships strained to the breaking point. And a dangerous drug ring poisoning an already toxic city. Another homerun by Creston Mapes!" — **Bestselling Author Diane Moody**

"I was quickly drawn into the story because, if Wayne Deetz is one of the first characters mentioned, I am in! I love how honest he is as a man, a police officer, and especially as a Christian. The story kept me reading and I didn't want to put it down. I loved the surprise visitor at the church and especially the ending. Thank you, Creston, for another wonderful story with characters who kept me reading!" — **Book Club Member Gail Mundy**

"If you love novels that deliver messages of hope, encouragement, and redemption this one is for you! This book is part of a series, and also serves as a standalone book. *Secrets in Shadows* was a page turner from the very beginning and did not disappoint! I hope to read many more parts to this series!" — **Lynnelle Murrell**

Scripture quotations from: *New American Standard Bible* (NASB) 1960, 1977, 1995 by the Lockman Foundation. *The Holy Bible,* New International Version (NIV) 1973, 1984 by International Bible Society.

The mission of Alcoholics Anonymous, Copyright © AA Grapevine, Inc.

The 12 Steps are from 'This is AA: An Introduction to the AA Recovery Program,' Copyright © 2017 by Alcoholics Anonymous World Services, Inc.

The AA poem read by Elmore in chapter 13 was written by Walter (Smitty) Smith, and credit is given to him for this beautiful work. No more information about the author or poem could be found.

Grateful for friend-author-cop Mark Mynheir for always being available to answer my questions about police procedures.

Thanks to the team at the Portland Police Bureau for answering my many questions about everything from training and wages to equipment, weapons, personnel, and procedures.

Special thanks to my early reader team for your time and insights: Patty Mapes (wink, wink), Gail Mundy, Diane Moody, Sharon Srock, Lynnelle Murrell, Rachel Savage, and Ginger Aster.

Thanks to The Closer, Chuck Pardoe, for his listening ear and creative input.

SECRETS
IN
SHADOWS

A Novel

1

___

For Portland Police Investigator Wayne Deetz to get a personal phone call after hours from Sergeant Dolby Tidwell was slightly unusual. Even though the two veterans of the Portland Police Bureau had been working behind the badge together for more than fifteen years and considered themselves close friends—even blood brothers while in the trenches—they rarely talked on the phone outside of work.

As Deetz drove down Tidwell's tree-lined street in suburban Cedar Mill, west of the city, he recalled when he had been to the sergeant's home—in good times and bad. Once he was there around Thanksgiving deep into the night for a rousing poker game among colleagues. Another time he was there for a somber afternoon reception following the funeral of fellow officer Lance Burke, Tidwell's closest friend.

Deetz had noticed lately that Tidwell had been short-tempered and irritable, two traits that were out of character for him. Over the years, Tidwell had proven himself to be rock solid day in and day out. He was cool, easygoing, and completely in charge, a strong and admirable leader.

Deetz had just assumed Tidwell was feeling the pressure and fallout from decisions made two years earlier by Mayor Barbara Meeks and Portland City Council to defund the police. As a result, the Bureau had been short several hundred officers. Not only that, because of the many volatile protests occurring almost nightly in the city, members of the Bureau's Rapid Response Unit had resigned in droves. Of course, when Portland's crime and murder rates skyrocketed over the course of the past two years, the powers that be voted to refund the police, causing Tidwell and the Bureau to scramble to rebuild the force. Currently, the Bureau was still a flag flying at only half-mast.

"I need to see you." That was all Tidwell had said when he'd phoned Deetz after work earlier that evening.

It was approaching 8:30 p.m. at the close of a picturesque July day in Portland, Oregon.

Deetz spotted Tidwell as soon as he pulled up the incline to the crest of his driveway. The big man was seated in a chair on his front porch wearing khaki shorts, a faded yellow tank top, and worn leather sandals. His massive, tan arms rested on the arms of the chair, and he held his trademark amber-colored bottle of Killian's Irish Red beer in one hand. Tidwell's lovely old Golden Retriever, Lady, was sprawled out at the big man's feet.

Deetz parked the Subaru near the sergeant's Dodge Charger, got out, and headed across the driveway and up the sidewalk. Lady stood and wagged her tail to greet him. Tidwell reached into the cooler next to him, pulled out a beer, twisted the top off, and set it on the wide arm of the chair next to him.

"What is going on, Sergeant?" Deetz said in a humorous tone as he climbed the steps, took the beer, and sat down in the chair next to Tidwell.

Tidwell said nothing and stared straight ahead at the lush green front yard that sloped down to the peaceful street.

"It's quiet around here," Deetz said, petting Lady and starting to feel a bit uncomfortable about why Tidwell had asked to see him. "Where is everybody?"

It hadn't dawned on Deetz until that moment that his job could be in jeopardy. Feeling a tingling of anxiety in his fingertips, he racked his brain for anything he'd done terribly wrong or stupid in the past few weeks. He wondered if it may have anything to do with the traumatic and highly publicized Newman-Dowdy murder case from two months earlier.

"Janet's gone," Tidwell said, still looking out over the yard.

"Oh? Where to?"

Tidwell frowned and shook his head. "Not sure. That's part of the reason I wanted to talk to you."

"Okay." Deetz took a sip of beer and tried to lean back and relax; thankful he wasn't being fired. "Talk to me. What's going on?"

The big man finally turned to face Deetz. "She said she needed *space*. Wanted to get out of town. She's probably at her sister's in Bend. I'm not sure." He tilted his head back, drained the bottle, set it in the cooler, and got another.

Deetz sipped his beer and waited.

Lady walked back over and laid down next to Tidwell.

"I've been losing my temper." Tidwell twisted the cap off the new beer, tossed it in the cooler, and slammed the lid shut. "And I've been drinking too much."

"Just beer, or—"

"Liquor, too. Gin. Bourbon."

"How much?"

"Enough to get me good and numb each night."

"Each night?"

"That's what I said."

"Does Janet drink with you?"

"She used to have a glass of wine at night, but she stopped that."

"What is—"

"She confronted me, told me my drinking was out of hand. She stopped drinking, I guess to make a point, or to encourage me to stop, or to set an example—I don't know."

Deetz took a moment to digest this before asking, "So, what do you think is causing the anger?"

"I have no idea, but I'm mad all the time. It's like there's a constant rage boiling underneath the surface. I'm uptight. On edge. I didn't used to be like this."

Tidwell took a big swig. Deetz knew it was awkward, but he waited for Tidwell to continue.

"Here's one for you," Tidwell said. "I ran a guy off the road on the way home." Tidwell leveled his gaze at Deetz as if to say, 'Can you believe that?'

"I was in a long line of cars in a right-turn-only lane—the one at

Brewster and Kennedy. I'd waited like five minutes to get to the light, and this dude in a Beamer comes flying up from way back and darts in right in front of me. I lost it, Wayne. I rode his rear like a maniac. Not only did I run him off the road, I got out of my Charger —with my gun."

Deetz shook his head and sighed, not believing what he was hearing from one of the top officials at the Portland Police Bureau.

"Luckily, I came to my senses and took off before I killed the guy."

Deetz frowned and sighed.

"I needed to talk to somebody. I feel like I'm losing it."

"Are you drinking during the day?" Deetz said.

"Not yet." Tidwell chuckled and stroked his bald head with a large hand. His face was dark and weathered from spending lots of time in his garden with Janet. But Deetz could see where he had aged—the blue eyes a bit sunken, the new lines engraved in his forehead.

"When you say anger, I mean, you haven't . . . done anything to Janet."

Tidwell huffed. "Come on, Wayne, you know me better than that."

Deetz waited.

"But we've been arguing all the time, about everything. Money. Relatives. Groceries. Credit cards. Where to set the thermostat— you name it, we argue about it. It's been like this for a few months now."

"That's not like you guys."

Tidwell and Janet had always seemed like the ideal couple, like best friends.

"Lately, she's been looking at her phone all the time. Social media. Games. I mean, does that sound like her? She always used to hate that stuff. She would make fun of it. Now we argue about how much time she spends on it. It's like I've turned her off so much she's resorting to her phone for interaction or entertainment or something."

"What's behind all this?" Deetz said. "What's causing your anger? Is it the pressure at work?"

"Some of it. That's been a nightmare, as you know. Maybe it's a bigger burden than I realize."

"I can understand that, man. You're under the gun, big time. You're trying to keep the city safe under a broken system. You're trying to hire hundreds of people back, plus help run the Bureau. There's a lot on your shoulders."

"But that's no excuse! I'm in that job because I'm supposed to be able to handle all that stress. I used to handle it fine."

"Yeah, but you're human—"

"It's not just that . . ." Tidwell's mouth sealed closed and he shook his head slightly.

"What else?" Deetz said.

Tidwell's eyes were suddenly glassy.

"Nick."

Nick was the Tidwell's only child. He would be twenty-four now, the same age as Deetz's son, Brandon, a rookie cop with the Portland Police Bureau, and Deetz's temporary partner. The last Deetz knew, Nick had been learning the heating and air trade, but that was a while back. He and Brandon had been friends for a season during their high school years.

"He's not good," Tidwell said. "You know he's an EMT—"

"No. How long's he been doing that?"

"A year. It's kicking his rear. A lot of times they have him working midnight to noon. They transport to Portland Memorial, if that tells you anything."

"Ouch. I can only imagine the calls he gets in that part of town."

Tidwell nodded. "Shootings, rapes, overdoses. A couple weeks ago he had to get a kid out of a car who had been shot in the back of the head execution style. His supervisor *made him* give the guy CPR."

"What?"

Tidwell nodded. "Nick told his supervisor the guy was obviously about to die any second. But the supervisor went by the book, made him do the CPR. Can you imagine? Idiot. Anyway, Nick is having PTSD issues . . . It's killing Janet."

"Is he getting counseling?"

"We've told him to. He said he tried it but it didn't help. He's drinking and doing who knows what else. I finally kicked him out of the house, told him to grow up. He was living here until a few months ago."

"Where's he living now?"

"He met a girl, an overnight nurse at the hospital. Jody. They're living together in Hayhurst. Nice girl. We were hoping she would be good for him; get him straightened out."

"Maybe that will happen."

Tidwell shook his head. "She called Janet yesterday. Said Nick's been missing work some. She thinks he's smoking crack or doing some kind of hard drugs. Been acting really weird—destructive. She told Janet she's moving out, or she's trying to get him to move out. She didn't realize how bad it was. She said he needs rehab. She wanted to give us a heads-up. Nick can't afford that place without her income. He'll probably come crawling back here."

"Man . . . I'm sorry." Deetz was deflated. These were heavy issues.

"Everything's just so . . . messed up. And I look at you. Your kids are solid. Your marriage is solid—"

"Dude, we have plenty of problems—"

"But you always take the high ground, Wayne. That's what I think of when I think of you. You're so . . . good."

Deetz laughed. "I'm not good, Dolby. I'm not. I promise you. I struggle just like everyone. If you see anything different in me, anything good, it's just God. You're seeing him, not me."

Tidwell winced and looked away. "I know you believe all that stuff." He paused. "I believe in God. But we've never gone to church. We never taught Nick about God. I feel like we've failed him."

"Look, you are where you are," Deetz said. "It sounds like you need to love Nick and get him the help he needs."

"He's an adult. My gosh. How long are we going to have to babysit him? Men today aren't men anymore. It's ridiculous. Grow up. Work. Take responsibility."

"You remember Callie Freeland? Well, she married Tyson Cooper so she's Callie Cooper now. You remember her?"

Tidwell nodded.

"She would know the best rehab places for Nick."

"Text me her info, will you?"

Deetz worked his phone out of his back pocket. "Also, J.P.'s girl-friend Tammy is a social-worker, she'll know some good places. She may have some connections."

Tidwell waved at Deetz's phone. "Hit me up."

"Okay, I'm sending you their contact info as we speak," Deetz said slowly, trying to type and talk at the same time. "Maybe I can ask Brandon to reach out to Nick. He found a really good group for young adults. He likes it a lot."

"Yeah, I mean, you'd need to warn Brandon that Nick's really rough around the edges right now."

"Okay," Deetz said. "I'm not making any promises. He has a girlfriend now. Met her at that group. So, all he's been doing is working and seeing her."

Tidwell shot a quick smile, but then his face fell again.

"So, what are you going to do about your marriage and the drinking?" Deetz said.

"No clue." Tidwell took another swig of his beer. "Just feels good to talk about it. Thanks for listening."

Deetz knew Tidwell needed Christ in his life—and the peace that only he could bring. And he needed a friend he respected to speak into his life.

"Let me ask you this, when you drink—let's say in excess some-times—what do you think you're searching for?"

Tidwell shook his head slightly then leaned back in his chair, sighed, and looked out over the front lawn. He shrugged. "Escape."

Deetz was quiet for a moment, then said, "From what?"

Tidwell threw up his hands. "Everything. The trouble with Nick, and Janet, and work . . . Life."

Deetz thought about it and said, "You're looking for peace, man. Contentment."

With his shoulders back, Tidwell continued staring out into the dark, his eyes glistening.

"Maybe you're searching for the capacity to cope with it all," Deetz said.

Tidwell nodded.

"Dolby, I know from firsthand experience, that's what a man finds when he's filled with God's spirit. When he gives his life to

God and invites God in—he finds peace of mind, he finds the capacity to cope, he finds fullness and satisfaction."

Tidwell looked over at Deetz and stared at him.

They were silhouettes in the night.

"I want that," Tidwell said softly.

Deetz contemplated how to respond and silently asked for God to give him the words.

Tidwell's phone buzzed. "Let me check this, Wayne, it could be the Bureau."

Tidwell got his phone out, checked the screen, glanced at Deetz, and stood abruptly. Lady looked up at him.

"Hey," he said, taking several steps. "What's up?"

With the phone to his ear, Tidwell swiveled to face Deetz with his mouth open, his eyes huge and concerned.

"Are you okay?" Tidwell's voice was filled with alarm.

While holding the phone, Tidwell felt his pockets and mouthed that he had to go.

"Where . . . where did this happen?" Tidwell said. "Where are you?"

Deetz stood, certain something bad had happened to Nick.

Lady stood.

"Okay, I know right where you are. And where is the blood coming from?" Tidwell dashed to the front door, let Lady inside, locked the door, and made giant strides across the porch and down the front steps.

"Okay, don't worry. Don't move, okay? Stay right where you are. You said someone's called an ambulance? Good, good. You're going to be okay, honey. I'll be there as fast as I can."

Deetz followed Tidwell down the steps. *It must be Janet.* He wondered if Tidwell would want him to go with him, or even drive him.

"Yes, I'll stay on with you. Hold on a second." Tidwell lowered the phone and looked back at Deetz. "Janet got hit. She's hurt. I think she's pinned in. I gotta go."

He got in the Charger and the car thundered to life.

"Do you want me to come?" Deetz mouthed the words.

Tidwell shook his head and roared down the driveway.

2

By the time Tidwell got to the scene of Janet's car accident, firefighters and paramedics had freed her from the driver's compartment and had her on a gurney being rolled to an ambulance.

Running toward the scene from where he'd parked at a nearby pharmacy, Tidwell was shocked at the damage done to Janet's dark blue VW Tiguan. It was demolished and folded up like an accordion from the rear. The driver's compartment was half its normal size, the seat was bashed forward, and the airbags were stained with blood. The windshield was cracked in several places.

How did she survive?

Tidwell clenched his teeth and breathed fire as he examined the white Mercedes that had hit her, which was now parked fifteen yards behind the Tiguan. Its front was destroyed, windshield also smashed, and airbags had been deployed. The driver's door was open and no one was in the car.

Two Portland Police vehicles were at the scene as well as two ambulances and a firetruck. Luckily, the evening rush hour was over and traffic wasn't as bad as it could have been.

Someone was being tended to in one of the ambulances and Tidwell assumed it was the driver who'd hit Janet.

Several Portland officers directed traffic with flashlights at the intersection, which was scattered with shattered glass, broken car parts, and puddles of strong-smelling fuel and radiator fluid. Firefighters had sprayed the area with foam and were cleaning up the debris.

"Hey, honey. Hey, babe. It's me." Tidwell ran up beside the quickly moving stretcher, out of breath. "Are you okay?"

He reached for Janet's free hand; the other hand and arm were in an inflatable sling. Her eyes were open, they did find him, but she did not react. One side of her face was covered in blood, and she was groggy and seemed to be fading in and out.

"Sir, please, give us room," barked one of three paramedics, a stocky male wearing a headlamp. "We need to transport her fast. Are you related?"

"Husband. What's wrong with her?" Tidwell said, his heart pounding. "What are her injuries?"

A female paramedic spoke up as she guided the stretcher and tried to keep an oxygen mask over Janet's mouth at the same time. "Multiple lacerations, broken arm, possible internal injuries. We think she may have a concussion. Please move, sir."

Janet's glazed eyes fixed on Tidwell, who nodded and tried to smile. "Everything's okay, babe. They're going to take good care of you."

Janet's expression was solemn. Her eyes rolled back in her head, but then she found Tidwell again and shook her head ever so slightly.

Somewhere in the back of Tidwell's mind he wondered what she was still doing in Portland. She'd said she needed space and was going out of town. He assumed she was going to be with her sister three hours away in Bend, or to be with friends in Salem or Eugene.

"Can I ride with her?" Tidwell said, as the team got Janet to the open doors at the rear of the ambulance.

The other ambulance roared to life and took off into the night.

"Against protocol, sir," said the third paramedic, a tall, thin Black guy, also wearing a headlamp. "But you can meet us at ER. We have her purse with us; we'll keep it with her."

"Look, I'm Sergeant Tidwell, Portland PB. Please, let me ride with my wife."

"Sir, we can't do that—"

"Give me a break! I'm riding with her!"

"Sir, if we need to get officers involved, we will," said the female paramedic, nodding toward Tidwell's colleagues.

"What are you saying? They work for *me!*" Tidwell blasted.

"Sir. You're being belligerent and you smell like you've been drinking." The stocky paramedic spoke up as they rolled and bumped Janet's stretcher into the vehicle. "Either stand down or we'll get one of your officers to give you a breathalyzer."

Whoa!

That stunned Tidwell, as if he's been cold-cocked. He stepped back.

"Can I be of assistance here?" came a male voice from behind.

Tidwell turned around and his eyes met those of a huge, extremely young Black cop Tidwell's size—six-foot, three-inches tall, about two-hundred twenty pounds. Tidwell recognized him. His name badge read, 'Waters,' and he shined his flashlight toward Tidwell.

"Sergeant Tidwell," the young officer said with surprise. "Can I help you, sir? I'm Officer Waters, by the way, Clarence Waters."

Waters was a rookie who'd come up through Basic Academy with Deetz's son, Brandon. They'd given him a nickname, something like Rock or Stone or something like that.

"No, Waters . . . Thanks." Tidwell dropped back from him so the young officer wouldn't smell his breath and nodded toward Janet. "That's my wife. I'm going to meet her at ER."

"Oh, by all means." Waters said. "Do you want me to take you . . . or I could escort your car?"

Tidwell withdrew even more. "That won't be necessary, Waters. Who's handling the accident report?"

"My partner, sir. Officer Rickert."

Oh, great.

Waters pointed toward the veteran officer whom Tidwell knew all too well. Harold Rickert had a rock-solid build and erect posture, with big wrists, and he wore his gray hair in a clean-cut flattop. Tidwell and Rickert had never gotten along. Rickert was serious, had a cold personality, and was as old school as they came. He'd had more than his fair share of run-ins with people of color, both citizens and those on the force.

Rickert had also been partnering with Tidwell's best friend,

Lance Burke, the night Lance had been gunned down in cold blood. Lance's killer had never been found and Tidwell had always been suspicious of Rickert's story from that night.

Just before the paramedics shut the back doors of the ambulance, Tidwell yelled to Janet that he would see her at the hospital. She lifted several fingers, but that was it.

Tidwell dashed over to Officer Rickert, who had just finished talking to a bystander, someone Tidwell assumed witnessed the accident.

"Rickert, hey." Tidwell approached but kept his distance. "I've got to get to the hospital so I'm in a hurry, but can you tell me what happened?"

"Hey, Sergeant. I saw it was your wife that got hit. Too bad," said Rickert, holding a clipboard against his broad chest.

"What do you have in the report? What happened?"

"Fool in daddy's Mercedes was looking down at his phone. Didn't even see your wife till he was eating the trunk of her car. I'll be citing him—if he makes it. His injuries are substantial. Serves him right."

Tidwell turned to head for his Charger.

"Daddy's got him insured to the teeth, so you're good there, Sergeant."

Tidwell nodded and took off.

It was going to be a long night.

The mention of possible internal injuries to Janet made Tidwell sick to his stomach.

He needed to let Nick know what was happening.

As he jogged toward his vehicle, Tidwell eyed Janet's smashed car and something pulled at him. She'd called him after she'd been hit. *What about her phone?* He veered and ran for her car.

The driver's side entry was unrecognizable. *How had she been able to call me?* Between the bent seat, the bloody airbag, and the cracked windshield, there was barely any room for a person to sit. He wondered how she'd survived. He got his phone out, turned on the flashlight, and searched the floor. No phone.

He dashed around to the passenger side, fought with the door, and finally pried it open. He pointed the light around the compressed interior. The passenger airbag had not deployed, but that side of the car had been crunched as well. Tidwell guessed this was where the paramedics found Janet's purse.

If she called him after she'd been hit, she couldn't have put the phone back in her purse. *It's either on her, or it's here somewhere.*

He frantically searched the floor and front interior. He got out and entered through the back door but found only an umbrella, a book, and water bottle. Then it dawned on him to ring Janet's phone.

Ahh.

The buzzing vibration sounded from the front part of the car. Tidwell hurried back around front, got on his knees, and stuffed his hands beneath the airbags and reached and patted all around.

Janet's phone stopped buzzing; it must have gone to voicemail. Tidwell cursed and pulled back with a grunt, dialed her number again, and listened. The buzzing began again and it was close by. With his huge upper body he forced the airbags upward and saw the light of Janet's pulsing phone.

He reached across and snatched it.

Good.

He got up fast, took one last look at the totaled car, and ran for his Charger.

Janet had not looked good.

He could only hope she was going to be okay.

Now this, on top of all the trouble with Nick.

It was starting to rain by the time Tidwell got to the Charger. He quickly got in, tossed Janet's phone on the passenger seat, started the car, and headed out of the parking lot toward the hospital.

The rain came harder and he flipped the wipers to a faster speed.

The city lights were blurred by the rain. Several people walking the town were caught in it and ran for cover beneath the awning of a pizza shop.

He wondered if Nick would be working tonight. If he might be able to come to the hospital. What kind of condition he would be in if he did?

Tidwell glanced toward Janet's phone on the seat next to him.

For perhaps the first time ever, he worried about what she might be hiding from him.

3

DEETZ'S WIFE Joanie and nineteen-year-old daughter Leena had insisted on going with Deetz to the hospital late that night. Over the past fifteen years the Deetz and Tidwell families had become close friends. Joanie and Janet always hit it off like old schoolmates, and Leena and the giant Tidwell had a special, sweet relationship. Leena was on the autism spectrum and Tidwell always went out of his way to connect with her; their relationship was special.

"How is she?" Deetz said to Tidwell as they approached him in the hospital's low-lit waiting area.

Tidwell stood from the chair in the corner, bent over, and gave Joanie a hug. Then he looked at Leena. "My word, young lady, you get more beautiful each time I see you!"

Leena laughed and shook her head; her cheeks turning pink. "Thank you, Sergeant Tidwell."

"Now I've told you before to call me Dolby, remember?"

Leena smiled and nodded. "Mom and Dad will probably make me call you Mister Dolby."

"No, no. No mister. It's just Dolby to you. It's mister to those brothers of yours!"

They all laughed.

Tidwell set his shoulders back and exhaled. "She's going to be okay. She has cuts and bruises on her legs and arms and chest. The impact was traumatic. The other driver didn't even slow down.

Luckily, they don't think there are serious internal injuries. She does have a concussion. And one broken arm."

"Oh Dolby, I'm so relieved she's okay," Joanie said.

"Did you get to see her?" Deetz said.

"Just for a few minutes. She's pretty shaken up. They're still doing some cognitive testing. I think she's still in shock."

"Does she get to go home tonight?" Leena said.

Tidwell smiled and rested a large hand atop Leena's shoulder. "I wish she could, Leena, but they are going to keep her here for at least one night so they can keep an eye on her. Probably a much better plan than having me take care of her."

"True, true," Leena said.

They all laughed and when Leena realized she'd made them chuckle, she grinned from ear to ear.

"Was the other driver hurt?" Deetz said.

Tidwell nodded. "In ICU right now."

"Is there anything we can do for you?" Joanie said.

"No, thank you," Tidwell said. "I've got the neighbor looking in on Lady. It's so nice you came, especially so late. I appreciate it."

"Have you been able to tell Nick?" Deetz said.

"I left him a voicemail." Tidwell threw up his hands. "That's all I can do. He rarely answers when I call him."

"Are you going to stay?" Deetz said.

"Yeah. Although the nurses didn't seem too crazy about having me around."

The Deetzes chuckled.

"They told me they're probably going to need to wake her up on and off throughout the night, just to make sure she wakes up normally—with the concussion and all."

"Maybe you should go home and get a good night's sleep," Deetz said. "She's in good hands."

"Wayne, really?" Joanie said in an exasperated tone. "He wants to be with her."

"Well, I'm just saying, the nurses are going to be in and out of there all night; he won't get any sleep."

"I'll stay if they let me," Tidwell said. "I don't want her to be alone."

"Well, you'll get 'Husband of the Year' if you do stay," Leena said in all seriousness.

Without realizing it, Leena always said just the right thing at the right time to make people laugh and to ease tensions. It never failed.

As the Deetzes were saying their goodbyes, Tidwell asked if Wayne could step aside and talk for a minute. Deetz wondered, hoped, Tidwell was going to want to talk more about what they'd been discussing on Tidwell's porch before Janet called.

"What's up?" Deetz said, as the two men wandered over toward the vending machines.

"I found Janet's phone—in her car." Tidwell leveled his gaze at Deetz.

"And?" Deetz said.

"From what I can tell, she was on her way to—"

"Dad!" came a loud male voice from down the hallway.

They all looked.

It was Nick Tidwell, taking giant strides toward them in his navy EMT uniform and black steel-toed boots.

Nick ignored Joanie, Leena, and Deetz and went straight to his dad.

"Where is she? Is she okay?" Nick was jumpy and out of breath.

Tidwell began to calm his son and explain Janet's condition.

Nick stood almost as tall as his dad but was extremely thin; thinner than Deetz remembered him. He had a ruddy face. His large brown eyes were bloodshot. His longish brown hair crept down his neck out the back of his navy EMT cap.

"I want to see her," he said, still not acknowledging the others.

"In a minute. Can you say hello to the Deetzes?" Tidwell sounded annoyed. "They came all the way down here to see how Mom is."

Nick sheepishly turned and said, "Hello Deetzes. Thank you for coming."

Nick had a small raw patch of skin on his left cheek and his teeth looked slightly discolored. He turned back to his dad. "What room? I've got to get back to work soon."

Rude.

Tidwell, obviously frustrated by his son's demeanor, mumbled something to him, and started walking toward Janet's room. Nick followed, nervously pulling up his pants and adjusting his jacket.

Tidwell looked back at the Deetzes. "Thank you all again for coming. When she gets better, we all need to get together."

Nick did not look back, but followed his dad with lanky, almost clumsy strides.

Deetz was frustrated Tidwell had not gotten to finish telling him what he'd found on Janet's phone. It had been rare for the big man to confide in Deetz in the first place. But now, with Nick in the picture and Janet needing care, Deetz was afraid he may have lost his chance to help Tidwell.

"Contact me any time, Sarge," Deetz called.

But Tidwell did not look back.

4

———

EARLY THE NEXT MORNING, as they'd been doing the past two months, Deetz met his son Brandon at the Portland Police Bureau. They saw each other briefly in the locker room and again at the coffee pot in the break room before the morning shift meeting. As Deetz had suspected, the de-brief was led by Investigator Virgil Bennett, who was filling in for Sergeant Tidwell.

Afterward, Deetz met Brandon at their patrol car, a black and white Ford Interceptor. With few words, Brandon settled into the driver's seat of the SUV and Deetz buckled into the passenger seat, both juggling coffee cups.

"Coat?" Brandon said.

"It's chilly," Deetz said.

"Clarence told me about Janet's accident last night," Brandon said as he started the SUV. "She going to be okay?"

"Yeah. How'd he know about it?" Deetz said.

"He and Rickert worked it."

Rookie officer Clarence Waters and Brandon had been room-mates since graduating from Basic Academy back in the spring. Clarence was being mentored by veteran officer Harold Rickert, while Deetz was mentoring Brandon.

"I didn't realize that," Deetz said. "Yeah, she's got cuts and bruises and a concussion, but she'll make it. Broken arm."

"You guys went to the hospital?" Brandon said.

"How do you know all this?" Deetz said.

"Leena texted me." Brandon laughed. "You can't get anything by me, Pops."

As Brandon maneuvered the car toward their assigned patrol zone on the east side of the city, Deetz silently acknowledged how thankful he was that Brandon had settled into the job so well after the tragic office shooting they'd worked on his first day in uniform back in May.

Ironically, the gruesome shooting had taken place at Brandon's brother's office complex downtown. Brandon and Deetz had been among the first on the scene at the offices of J.P.'s coffee company, where Brandon ended up gunning down the shooter, a mentally disturbed man named Greg Newman. Quite a bit of mental trauma followed, as two people lost their lives, others were injured, and Christopher Dowdy and his father, Alexander, received multiple felony charges.

Brandon had been to see a Bureau psychiatrist several times a week following the incident. Now he visited with her once a month. He insisted he was fine and the only reason he was still seeing Dr. Terri Wallender was because the middle-aged woman was apparently so drop-dead gorgeous.

"Yeah," Brandon broke the silence, "Clarence said Sarge got pretty heated when the EMTs wouldn't let him ride in the ambo."

"Oh, really?" Deetz said, more curious than surprised.

"Yeah, Clarence said he kind of had to defuse the situation."

"Well, that's good." Deetz didn't want to defend Tidwell if he'd been unruly. "So how are Clarence and Rickert getting along these days? Any better?"

"Far from it," Brandon said. "Clarence can't stand him. He can't wait till field training is over and he gets a new partner."

"What's the main problem?"

"Rickert just sounds like a total jerk. First of all, he's clearly prejudiced. He'll make under-his-breath comments about Blacks right in front of Clarence. And about Hispanics, Asians, gays—anyone who's not a grouchy old white guy like him. Clarence just fumes. Rickert's lucky Clarence hasn't flattened him yet."

"I told you, Rickert's as old school as they come."

"Old school is one thing . . . Oh hey, by the way, what's the story behind what happened with Rickert and his partner who died, you know, Sergeant Tidwell's buddy . . ."

"Lance Burke."

"Right. They were partners. How did Burke die? Wasn't there some mystery behind it?"

"Kind of. They'd been together about a year," Deetz said. "Lance never cared too much for Rickert; said he was a hot head. That's between us. Tidwell told me that. Anyway, it was a night shift. They were actually in Bridgepark, just a few blocks from here." Deetz pointed in that direction with coffee cup in hand. "Rickert said they were patrolling and came across what he called a 'gang' of seven Black kids hanging around outside the front of an abandoned theater."

Brandon listened intently and sipped his coffee as he continued driving east on I-84.

"Rickert was driving. His report says he pulled up next to the boys, parked, and he and Lance got out and approached the group to disperse them. The report says Lance told the boys they were loitering and they needed to break it up and clear out. Then, Rickert said, a shot was fired. He said it came from behind the boys, in the shadows near the front doors of the theater. The bullet hit Lance in the neck; he died almost instantly."

Deetz fought back his emotions and paused, with Brandon glancing over at him.

"The boys scattered. Rickert drew his weapon. But when he saw how bad Lance was hit, he made it over to him, called it in, and tried to stop the bleeding. While he was working on Lance, he saw a kid with a gun run away from the shadows where the shot came from."

"The shooter was never caught?" Brandon said.

"Nope."

"Weapon?"

"Never found."

"What kind of gun?"

"Thirty-eight."

"Wasn't there some controversy over what really happened that night?" Brandon said.

"How do you know this?" Deetz said.

Brandon chuckled. "I heard you and Tidwell talking about it one time."

The car was silent as Deetz debated how much, if any, to share with his son.

"This is between us, you got me? You don't tell Clarence this, or anyone."

"Sure, yeah."

"The autopsy on Lance indicated the shot came from closer range," Deetz said. "Rickert estimated it at twenty yards when the autopsy estimated it at more like six to eight yards."

"Really."

"Also, after it happened . . ." Deetz stopped and debated whether to say any more.

"After it happened . . ." Brandon coaxed him.

"Rickert had a bandage on his ear for quite a while afterward."

"Meaning what? That something else happened that he didn't put in the report?"

"Again, this is between us, Son. I have your word on that, right?"

"Yes, Dad, come on."

"The rumor was it was a bite mark—on his ear."

Deetz vividly remembered sitting in his patrol car a day or two after Lance died. It was cold and drizzly. He'd pulled up and parked next to Assistant Head of Homicide Sid Sikorski, who was in his unmarked car, with Sergeant Tidwell riding shotgun. Sid told Deetz he'd seen Rickert in the locker room that morning. The bandage on Rickert's ear had come off and he was slightly frantic trying to get a new one on before anyone saw it. Sid swore it looked exactly like a bite mark.

"Dad—did you hear me?"

Deetz snapped out of the daze. "No, sorry. What?"

"What do you think really happened?" Brandon said as he took the Concord Avenue exit ramp.

"Maybe one of the boys in the group had a gun. Maybe there was an altercation. We just don't know."

"What about the MAV cam?" Brandon said, referring to the Mobile Audio and Video (MAV) recording system installed in all Portland Police cruisers.

"That's another mystery," Deetz said, rehashing it in his mind. "Rickert really should have pointed the car toward the group of boys when he parked so it would be on MAV, but he didn't."

"That's textbook."

"I know." Deetz shook his head. "The car was facing off to the side."

"We need body cams."

"Yeah . . . I'm still up in the air on that one."

"They're coming," Brandon said.

"They've been saying that forever."

"So really, only Rickert and those boys know what happened—what really happened," Brandon said.

"That's true, unless by chance anyone else was watching."

"Did Rickert get in trouble—for not facing the MAV camera toward the group?"

"No. No way. He's a veteran. Plus, his excuse was that he didn't want to point his headlights on them for fear they would scatter before he and Lance could talk to them. So he eased the car over to the side for a more friendly approach. It could all be legit."

"You don't believe that."

Deetz sighed. "It's tough. I know Tidwell wrestles with it. I try not to judge. God knows what happened. I try to leave it with him."

5

WHEN TIDWELL OPENED his eyes after what felt like a long nap in Janet's bright hospital room, a doctor he didn't recognize was sitting next to her on the bed, quietly examining her.

Tidwell rubbed his eyes, sat up in the small chair in the corner of the room, and checked his watch: 8:15 a.m.

"Look at my light," the doctor said. "Follow it with your eyes."

The physician had a small frame and was slightly hunched. He was perhaps sixty-five with thinning black hair and old-fashioned silver glasses.

He must have tilted Janet's bed up. She was laying upright against her pillows and was slowly following his instructions.

"How does your head feel?" he said.

"It hurts. I'm sore," Janet said quietly. "My whole body aches."

Janet had a bandage high up on her forehead, and others on her arms. Her left arm was in a sling.

"Do you know what day it is?"

Janet closed her eyes and paused. Finally, she said Friday.

"Good. Can you tell me the date?"

"July twenty-second."

"Very good, Janet," he said. "With your right hand, can you reach up with a fist and push my hand?"

Janet slowly did as he said.

"Push my hand as hard as you can," he said.

She pushed it harder but closed her eyes and sighed in frustration.

"That was good," he said. "Are you nauseous at all?"

Janet shook her head slightly and mumbled "no," then turned her head toward where Tidwell was sitting.

"You're doing great, honey," Tidwell said, remaining in the chair.

Without looking at Tidwell, the doctor said, "Who is that over there?"

Tidwell opened his eyes wide and smiled and waved behind the doctor's back. For now, he would keep his questions about her phone and her whereabouts the previous night to himself.

"My goofy husband."

"Okay. And what is his name?"

"Dolby Tidwell."

"How long have you two been married?"

Without missing a beat, Janet said, "Almost thirty years."

"When is your husband's birthday?"

"January seventeenth."

Good.

"Can you touch your nose with your right index finger for me?"

Janet thought about it a second and did so.

"Good," the doctor said. "Your CT scan looked clean. Do you feel up to going home today?"

She closed her eyes and nodded. "Very much."

He nodded and patted her wrist. "I'm going to continue you on the acetaminophen for pain relief. You can take the maximum dosage on that, but I don't want you taking any other pain relievers because they can increase the risk of bleeding. You're going to need physical and mental rest for your brain to recover from the trauma it sustained. Just take it slow for the next few days, no intense workouts or screen time. You don't play video games, do you?"

They chuckled and the doctor and Tidwell stood up at the same time. Tidwell towered over him.

"Thank you very much, doctor." Tidwell reached out and shook the doctor's hand. "What is your name?"

"I'm sorry. Dr. Harlow, Winston Harlow." He patted around in the pocket of his white lab coat and handed Tidwell his card. "If there are any problems with memory, severe pain, vision, balance—you call me."

"What about her arm?" Tidwell said.

"It turned out to be a sprain. The sling will help. She can take it off when she feels ready to, probably in about a week or ten days."

Tidwell saw him out and returned to Janet's bedside. He bent down and kissed her forehead and ran his large hand through her straight brown hair. Then he pulled a chair over and sat down next to her.

"Is Lady okay?" Janet said.

Tidwell nodded. "Fine. George is watching her." He reached over and touched her shoulder. "I'm thankful you're okay. Your car was demolished."

Janet's dry lips squished into a frown, her eyes squeezed closed, and she began to cry softly.

"Hey, hey." Tidwell stood and leaned in close to her. "It's okay. Everything's okay."

He explained how she'd been hit from behind and that the young driver was in ICU. He told her the Deetzes had come by, which made her cry even more. For an instant, Tidwell recalled the talk he and Deetz had been having when Janet called him.

"Nick was here. Do you remember?" Tidwell said.

"Really? No . . . no, not at all."

"You were out of it."

"How was he?"

"Eh. Nick is Nick, what can I say? I was surprised he even showed up."

"I'm surprised *you* showed up," Janet said.

Tidwell's head craned back, and he squinted at her in disbelief.

That hurt.

And it angered him.

"I'm sorry," she whispered and reached for his hand.

But he pulled it away.

"Dolby, I'm sorry. I'm a mess right now. Forgive me. Just get me out of here. Please."

Tidwell stood abruptly. "Let me go find a nurse. I'll get you home asap."

He headed for the door.

"Hey," she called.

He stopped and turned around.

"Where's my purse . . . and phone?"

Tidwell said nothing, walked to the closet, and slid the wooden door open. He picked up the purse, knowing the phone was in it, and took it to her. He set it on the bed next to her.

"The phone's in there," he said. "You want me to tilt the bed up more?"

"That would be great."

While he did so, he struggled with whether this was the time to address what Janet had been doing the day before, where she was going, whom she was meeting? After all, she'd just had a traumatic car crash.

"That's good, right there," she said, about the height of the bed.

Tidwell removed his thumb from the button and made the decision to leave. He would address the phone with her later, at home. He gave her a peck on the forehead and started for the door.

"Who found this anyway?" she dropped a hand on her purse.

He turned around to face her. "Paramedics found the purse . . . I found your phone in your car."

Janet stared at him with her mouth open. They locked eyes for five seconds. It felt as if she was examining his face for any indication he may have looked at the device.

"The paramedics told me they had your purse," Tidwell said, "but on my way to my car I remembered you'd called me. I didn't want to leave your phone. I dug around under the airbags until I found it."

Her eyes widened and she nodded, not taking her eyes off him. Then, as if snapping out of a daze, she searched around in the purse and pulled out the phone. "Wow. I can't believe it's not cracked."

She powered it on.

"I don't even remember calling you."

Her brown eyes glowed from the reflection of the screen.

This was not the time or the place for what Tidwell was sure was going to be an explosive discussion.

"Okay, let me find out what we need to do to get you out of here." Tidwell turned and headed out. "I'll be back in a minute."

"Wait, Dolby . . . did you look at my phone?"

He just kept going.

6

As DEETZ and Brandon left the cluttered and disgusting two-bedroom townhouse in High Falls where they'd just calmed down a heated domestic dispute, Deetz wondered what Brandon must be thinking.

During Brandon's first two months on the job, he'd intervened in everything from office shootings and carjackings to prostitute rings and big-time drug deals.

"That was just plain sad," Deetz said as they got back into the Interceptor.

"I don't see how anyone can live like that. I can't get the smell out of my nose," Brandon said.

From what Deetz could tell, the odor Brandon spoke of had been a blend of cat litter, dog dander, and rotting food, which had been left out all over the residence, in all shapes and forms.

"They should let those Pitbulls out of their kennels once in a while to clean up all that food," Deetz said.

"That guy is a time bomb," Brandon said. "I wouldn't let my daughter near someone like that."

Deetz shook his head and reflected on how thankful he was to have been raised in a solid family and to have a wonderful wife like Joanie.

"Did I tell you Kristen doesn't have a dad?"

Brandon was referring to his new girlfriend, Kristen Trent,

whom he met just six or eight weeks ago at a small group for young adults.

"Yeah, you mentioned that," Deetz said.

"She told me when she looks at our family she can't believe how lucky I am."

Kristen had come over to the house two or three times, including once recently for a fourth of July celebration with family and close friends.

"What happened?" Deetz said. "When did her dad leave?"

"She was only one. She doesn't remember him and he's never reached out to her."

"Wow. Do they know where he is?"

"No. They don't want to know."

They rode in silence for a bit.

"My point was, she never had a dad to teach her all the things you've taught us." Brandon's voice broke slightly. "She never had parents who stayed married through the highs and lows. She said she didn't know families like ours even existed."

"We're lucky, Son."

"I'm thankful," Brandon said.

"Me, too."

Deetz's phone buzzed in his pocket. He got it out and looked at the screen. It was a text from Tammy, son J.P.'s girlfriend—the social worker. He read it silently:

> Hi Wayne. Sgt Tidwell reached out to me. I told him about a 30-day inpatient rehab for Nick called Redeeming Recovery but wait times can be long. Also told him about The Morning 7s, an addiction recovery group that meets at 7am seven days a week at Peace Gardens in Wicker. Wanted to keep you in the loop. Have a great day.

"Who's that?" Brandon said, looking over at Deetz's phone.

"Tammy," Deetz said. "Did I tell you I was at Tidwell's house last night when Janet called and told him she'd been in the accident?"

"No. What's that have to do with Tammy?"

"I'm getting to that. So, the reason Tidwell had me over, well, one of the reasons, was about Nick."

"Uh oh."

"Did you know he's a paramedic now?"

"Oh, wow. No."

"Yeah. He's had the overnight shift at Portland Memorial, so you can imagine the types of calls he's had to respond to. Anyway, some have been so horrific that he's suffering from PTSD. He's not doing well. Tidwell thinks he's also on drugs of some kind."

Brandon shook his head and kept his eyes on the road. "Nick's always been out there, Dad. He's a wild child."

"Have you been in touch with him at all?"

"It's been at least nine months, a year."

"What would you think about reaching out to him?" Deetz said, knowing it was going to be a tough sell.

"That would look pretty strange, contacting him out of the blue."

"I was thinking that group you've been going to might be good for him," Deetz said.

Brandon grimaced and strained his neck. "I don't think he'd fit in, Dad. It's basically a Bible study. I mean, I don't even think he's a believer . . ."

"Right. Well, I just thought I'd mention it. You were fairly close with him at one time, weren't you?"

"I wouldn't say 'close.' We hung out some in high school. We had a similar big group of friends."

They cruised a bit more in silence.

Deetz would drop the matter of Nick. He'd mentioned it and it would be up to Brandon to follow up or not. Deetz understood, either way.

"You getting hungry?" Deetz said.

"I could eat," Brandon said.

"I got an idea—"

"I know what you're going to say."

Deetz laughed. "What?"

"You're going to say, 'Let's cruise through Edgewood and eat at Taco Grande after.'"

Deetz laughed again and Brandon shook his head.

Edgewood was a tough, dark area. Lots of drugs, gangs, and crime. Lots of addiction. Oregon itself had the second-worst drug addiction rate of any state in the country, just behind Montana, and Deetz was convinced Edgewood was the birthplace of it all.

"You want to go down Fallmoth?" Brandon said, perking up in the driver's seat.

"Yeah, that's good," Deetz said, cherishing the thought of the mouth-watering tacos.

Just then, a dark blue Chevy sedan in front of them swerved over the center line, then back into its lane. It was going well under the speed limit.

"Whoa! Did you see that?" Brandon said.

"Sure did."

"Should we light him up?" Brandon said.

There appeared to be two people in the car—a tall driver and a short passenger. There were no other cars in sight.

Deetz hesitated, wondering if the car might lead them to a drug house. "Let's drop way back and follow. See where they go. If they were speeding we'd take them. But there's hardly any traffic and they're going slowly."

"Roger that," Brandon said.

7

THAT MORNING AT THE HOSPITAL, Tidwell had pretended not to hear Janet when she'd asked if he'd looked at her phone, and he'd quietly exited the room without a response. When he had returned to help her get dressed and prepare to be discharged, she asked again. He'd looked at her point blank and said, "I did look at your phone, Janet. But this is no place to discuss it. There are going to be nurses in and out of here for the next twenty minutes. Let's talk about it at home."

And now it was approaching noon and they were home.

Lady greeted them both enthusiastically. After Janet loved on the dog for a few minutes, Tidwell let her out in the back yard instructing her to do her business.

Neither Tidwell nor Janet had said more than a few words on the drive back to the house, or when getting Janet situated, because they both knew a dark storm was brewing between them.

She insisted Tidwell set her up in the guest bedroom down the hallway from their bedroom because she didn't want to keep him up at night as she tossed and turned with the sling on her arm. Plus, she wanted to be able to nap on and off, and the smaller room was toward the back of the house, away from everything.

Tidwell had quietly agreed and was determined to serve her the best he could. But the topic of her phone was a disquieting cloud hanging over them, and it needed to be addressed.

Janet was resting and Tidwell was heating up a can of soup in the kitchen. His plan was to discuss the phone calmly over lunch.

Just then, she walked slowly into the kitchen in her moccasins. She wore jeans and a casual beige top. "We need to talk." She pulled one of the bar stools out at the kitchen island and sat.

Tidwell stirred the soup, turned the burner all the way down, and joined her at the island. He stood, with his large hands resting on the countertop.

"So, you looked at my phone," Janet said. "What did you see?"

"First of all," Tidwell said, "I thought you were going out of town—to see Becky, or Kisha and Sam . . ."

He watched for her reaction, but she just stared at him with no expression and said nothing.

Tidwell continued. "So, when you called after you got hit and I realized you were still in town—"

"I said I needed *space*. I didn't say where I was going."

"You said you wanted to get out of town," Tidwell blurted.

"So, what did you see on the phone? Just spit it out."

"That, whoever it was you were texting was going to be late meeting up with you."

"And, what else?" Janet sassed. "What else did you snoop around and find?"

"Don't put this on me!" Tidwell felt his blood pressure rising. "This is *your* secret meet-up. I read the thread, Janet. All that was there. It looked like you deleted a lot of it. I'm not the one who owes the explanation here. Why don't you tell me where you were going and who you were meeting? That's fair enough, isn't it? I am your husband. There are no secrets, right?"

"I can't believe you looked at my phone. That's an invasion of my privacy. Since when do we do that to each other?"

"You can say that all day long, but it's an obvious cover-up. Who's really in the wrong here? Huh? Whoever you were planning to meet, it sounded pretty juicy—"

"What's that supposed to mean?"

"I think your words in the text were, 'I can't tell you how badly I need to get out of here.'"

"So what? I told you that myself!"

"Who is it, Janet? Is it a man?" With those words, Tidwell's emotions spilled over; his heart ached just saying it.

"I don't think I owe you an explanation."

"Really. You told this person you need space to breathe and think."

"Again, I told you that myself!"

"Whoever it was made dinner reservations," Tidwell said.

Janet stared at him as if shellshocked.

"It was a 'surprise' where it was going to be. How do you think I'm supposed to take that, Janet? Huh? How would that make *you* feel if you found those secrets on my phone?"

"That wouldn't happen because I would never secretly look at your phone. Never."

"So, I looked at your phone. I'm guilty. There's a lot bigger trespass going on here than that."

Janet dropped her head, shook it, and mumbled something Tidwell didn't understand.

"You said, 'I can't wait to see you,'" Tidwell said. "Just tell me who it is. How long's it been going on? I can take it."

Tidwell's heart hammered. He felt like he was standing on the edge of a cliff, waiting to be pushed.

"My head hurts," Janet said, still looking down. "I can't do this."

Tidwell cussed and spun away. He took two giant steps to the refrigerator, grabbed a beer, slammed the door, and stalked through the house toward the back door—hearing Janet's words just as he left the house.

"That's right, drink it all away."

8

BRANDON HAD DROPPED down to a speed of only twenty miles an hour in order to stay well back from the dark Chevy sedan that was creeping through Edgewood.

"Why do you think he's going so slow?" Brandon said.

"He may have spotted us," Deetz said with his eyes glued to the car. "I'm not sure. If they're on meth they're hyper-paranoid."

Brandon and Deetz slowly cruised past a slew of homeless people sitting, sleeping, and meandering through a muddle of sagging tents, shopping carts, wilting boxes, and lawn chairs.

The homeless community never ceased to render Brandon speechless. He knew many were mentally ill or addicted to drugs and alcohol, and some were just down and out on their luck. He felt grieved as he took in their scattered coolers and bicycles, wood crates and propane tanks, power cords and slow cookers, bulging plastic bags, laundry baskets, scooters, sleeping bags, and blankets.

"You know J.P. and Tammy volunteer at a soup kitchen around the corner," Deetz said.

"I knew they did that; I didn't know it was here."

"Yeah, it's a block over, on Cloverleaf."

"Tammy's amazing," Brandon said, as his thoughts turned to his new girlfriend, Kristen.

"I know. She works all day with the underprivileged, then she volunteers in her free time," Deetz said.

"Who does that?" Brandon said.

"I guess someone who really understands love," Deetz said. "She thinks of others before herself."

Brandon nodded and put on his blinker. The Chevy had made a left. He noticed a huge dent and white scrapes on the left rear passenger door and fender.

Brandon's folks had met Kristen several times, but he didn't really have a good read on what they thought of her. They were probably tapping the brakes, waiting to see if the relationship would last. *They may have reservations about her home life and background.*

Kristen had an unsettling childhood. After her dad left when she was a baby, her mom took to alcohol and went through a number of relationships with men, none of which lasted. In fact, most of them proved toxic. As a result, Kristen's personality was serious and reserved; she was extremely slow to let anyone get close to her. That's why it was unusual she'd attended the young adult group. She wasn't a Christian and had no experience with church or religion.

Her first night at the group was also Brandon's first night. For the icebreaker, they'd been paired together and forced to ask each other prescribed questions to get to know one another. Brandon smiled as he recalled how solemn she'd been. But, man, she was beautiful: long dark blond hair, tan, swimmer's shoulders, big brown eyes, and, when you could get a smile, it was haltingly attractive.

Suddenly, the Chevy, now about eighty yards in front of them on a narrow backstreet, swerved way right, splashed through puddles, and just missed a power pole before jerking back onto the road.

"That's it," Deetz turned on the lights and siren. "Pull him over, Son."

Brandon cleared his head and accelerated. The Interceptor roared to life and was on the Chevy's bumper within seconds.

Brandon's heart pumped.

The Chevy veered to the right side of the road and eased to a stop.

"Want me to take it?" Brandon said.

Deetz looked into his son's eyes for a good five seconds, then examined the Chevy. The driver was still and so was the passenger.

Just like with J.P. and Leena, Deetz was learning to trust God with Brandon's life and safety. This was even trickier because the kid was a Portland cop. He would be in danger almost daily; Deetz knew from first-hand experience. Sometimes, the thought of it was a tidal wave that overwhelmed him. But this was all part of the journey—having enough faith to let the boy go and to trust God's plan for him.

"Okay," Deetz nodded with confidence.

"You'll run the plates, right?" Brandon unbuckled, opened his door, and jumped out.

"Hey," Deetz called.

Brandon leaned over and looked in at his dad.

"I'm getting out and dropping back, you're talking to the driver. The car's the coffin, remember?" Deetz said. "If they try something with you, I've got to be out there, able to move, draw my weapon— I can't do that from inside the car. Always, always remember that."

Brandon inhaled deeply, nodded, and exhaled. "Got it."

"Don't get too excited on your first enlistment," Deetz said. It was an old saying he'd used with all the kids, reminding them to keep their cool.

Deetz exited the vehicle, closed his door, put a hand on the grip of his gun, and nodded for Brandon to do the same.

"I'll be right here," Deetz stopped at the front of the police car.

With hand on Glock, Brandon approached the dark Chevy.

Dirty windows.

No one was in the back seat and the driver's window was all the way down.

A thin, pale female with stringy brown hair, wearing a navy hoodie, was in the driver's seat gripping the steering wheel with skinny white hands.

"Good day," Brandon said. "May I see your driver's license and registration, please?"

The girl glanced at Brandon nervously, her shifty eyes under-lined by purple half-circles. Her lips were chapped, and her mouth had several nasty sores around it.

The passenger was the complete opposite—small, husky dark-skinned male sunk way down in the seat with a mean expression on his stone face. He wore a sleeveless white T-shirt, and was covered in smudged, poor-quality tattoos. He was strapping. Not an ounce of fat on him. His black hair was buzz cut and he had on tight faded jeans and black work boots.

The interior of the car was littered with fast food cups and wrappers, as well as baby bottles, empty energy drink cans, diapers, and other trash. Brandon saw no weapons, but he was leery of the passenger.

The girl had her wallet in her lap and her fingers trembled as they tip-toed through the various pockets. Finally, she handed her license to Brandon with a shaky hand, as if she was freezing cold.

He glanced at the license. The girl in the photo looked much younger and much healthier. Her name was Deborah Fugate and her address was in Washington state.

"Registration?" Brandon said.

"I . . . I can't find it," Deborah said, without looking at him.

"Is this your car?" Brandon said.

"Look, man, what's this about?" the passenger said in a belligerent tone. "We weren't speeding. Why'd ya'll pull us over? You've got to have a reason."

The passenger's eyes were black and the scowl etched on his face told Brandon he was trouble.

"Is this your car, Deborah?" Brandon said.

She nodded fast and mumbled yes.

"Is it insured?" Brandon said.

This time she only nodded and said nothing.

"Can you tell me why you swerved back there—when you barely missed that pole?"

The passenger shifted exaggeratedly in his seat and mumbled what jive this was.

"I'm sorry," Deborah said. "I must have been looking at my phone. I know I shouldn't do that."

The passenger shook his head, looked out his window, and let out a string of expletives.

"It's illegal in Oregon to drive while holding or using a cell phone—"

"I'm sorry. Please. Please give me a warning. I won't do it again. I wasn't going over the speed limit, I know that."

Brandon glanced back at his dad who still had his hand on his weapon and a serious look on his face.

Brandon knew the cell phone usage while driving would be a class B violation because she hadn't caused a crash, but it would still cost her a thousand bucks. *That would be a lot for the poor girl. There may be a baby involved.* He felt sorry for her.

He could ticket her for driving without registration and/or failure to maintain a single lane. He didn't know which violation would cost less. He debated what to do.

"What's it gonna be, big-shot?" said the passenger.

That's it.

Brandon leaned into the car and pointed at the passenger. "You, get out. Out of the car."

Deborah looked at the passenger, who whined exaggeratedly and threw his door open.

"Slow!" Brandon yelled.

Deetz came toward them quickly, hand still on his holstered weapon.

Brandon hurried around the back of the vehicle.

The passenger was out in a flash. His body looked as solid as a statue.

"I didn't do nothing!" he said, cussing a blue streak.

"Put your hands on the hood of the car and spread your legs wide," Deetz commanded as he approached the muscular man. "Keep an eye on the girl," he told Brandon.

Deborah was looking down at her phone, texting away at lightning speed.

"Stay off the phone," Brandon told her.

She nodded nervously, finished a few more words, sent the text, and tossed the phone into a compartment between the seats.

Deetz began to pat the man's arms and upper body.

Brandon, who was about six feet away, asked the driver if she would give him consent to search the car.

She looked over at him, her mouth gaping. "You're . . . you're asking permission?"

"No!" the passenger yelled while being searched. "The answer is no."

Deborah shook her head no.

39

"Watch it, man!" the passenger yelled at Deetz, who was patting down his mid-section.

Without a word, Deetz ripped a plastic bag from the front waistband of the man's jeans. He held it up and examined the contents of the bag and said, "That right there gives us permission to search the car, big-shot."

The man cursed and straightened, but Deetz shoved him back onto the car, then tossed the bag to Brandon and continued the pat down.

The bag contained a palm-sized chunk of what looked like a jagged clump of glass; Brandon assumed it was crystal meth, better known on the streets as ice.

"What else do you have?" Deetz said slightly out of breath as he continued patting down the man's thighs and calves.

It was times like these that Brandon worried about his dad, his age—dealing with thugs like this; especially this guy, who resembled a wild bull ready to bust out of his chute at any moment.

"Jesse!" Deborah's yell surprised Brandon.

He turned to her, remembering his dad had told him to watch her.

Gun!

Everything flicked to slow motion.

The passenger lurched away from Deetz, who stepped back and began to draw his weapon.

Brandon went for his Glock.

"Throw it!" the passenger yelled.

Deborah tossed the gun through the open door, toward the man's outstretched hands.

9

WHILE DRINKING the beer and brushing Lady in the back yard, Tidwell got more and more worked up and finally headed back inside to face off with Janet again.

He had to know who she'd been planning to meet.

If she's having an affair . . .

When he got to the kitchen, she was gone.

Probably lying down.

He set the bottle in the recycle bin and walked quietly down the hall to the guest bedroom. The door was shut. He reached a backward fist up to knock and stopped. He heard her muffled voice.

He put his ear to the door.

Lady was right at the door too, wagging her tail, and Tidwell put a finger to his lips and told her, "Shhh."

"I'll be fine," Janet said quietly. "The sling is a nuisance . . . I just need to take it slow for a few days."

Silence.

"There's nothing you can do . . . just wait for me. I'll be back at full strength in a few weeks . . . I don't know . . . You've got to admit it's pretty freaky this happened. It's like things were jinxed."

Tidwell's face burned and he could feel the blood pounding through his veins. It took everything in his power not to bust in the room.

"No, I mean, the one time we try to meet, and I get hit on the way?" Janet says.

I can't believe this is happening.

"You're probably right. But I've got to be careful, really careful. Dolby looked at my phone last night, after the accident . . . No, but he knows something's going on."

Janet had always been so faithful. Tidwell was thinking this must be a terrible dream. It had never entered his mind that she would cheat on him.

"Well, that's sweet of you," she said. "I just can't make any promises right now—"

Tidwell threw the door open and charged to the bed where Janet was lying on her back beneath the covers. The blinds were closed but the mid-day light filtered in around the edges.

Janet froze with her mouth gaping open and her eyes enormous.

Tidwell grabbed the phone and put it to his ear. "Who is this?" he demanded.

There was only silence on the other end.

Janet protested.

Lady glanced back and forth at them with a look of concern.

"Who is this?" Tidwell yelled.

"How dare you, Dolby!" Janet yelled. "Give me that." She began to get up, but Tidwell guided her back down, not wanting to make her injuries worse.

"Just stay there," he said through clenched teeth.

He crossed to the other side of the room and addressed the caller again. "I will find out who you are, and I will hurt you. Do you understand me?" Just as he was about to threaten the caller further, he heard a click.

Furious, Tidwell began tapping away at Janet's phone. Her texts had been cleared. Her recent calls had been cleared, except this one. He recognized the phone number; it was the same as that of the person she was supposed to have met up with the day before.

With the phone in his hands, he turned to Janet.

"Is this an affair? Just answer me, yes or no."

"I haven't done anything, Dolby, I swear."

"Is it a man? *Who?*" he roared.

"I have not done anything—"

"What do you call that conversation you just had?" He mimicked her: 'That's sweet of you . . .'"

Janet tossed the covers aside and groaned as she sat up in the bed. She was still fully dressed, her arm in the twisted sling. "All it's been is talk." She shook her head. "It's an old classmate. You don't know him."

Him!

Lady went over and nudged Janet with her nose to be petted, but Janet ignored her.

Tidwell stood stunned for a moment, as if bashed in the head with a bat. He saw stars. He shook his head. He looked down at the phone and hit the button to redial the guy's number. He put the phone to his ear.

"You're never here," Janet pleaded and started to cry. "You're married to the Portland Police Bureau."

Someone on the other end answered but said nothing.

Tidwell paused, listened to the silence, felt his pulse pounding in his head. "Whoever you are, you're a coward," he said. "You better go chase someone else's wife or you're going to find yourself *dead!*"

Tidwell was about to slam the phone onto the bed when it buzzed in his hand. He looked at the screen hoping the guy's name or photo would come up, but instead, it was his son Nick's picture; one from several years ago in which he was smiling and looking twenty-five pounds heavier than he'd looked the night before.

"It's your son." Tidwell spiked the phone onto the bed and stalked out.

"Would you come back here? Dolby, come back," Janet said. "We need to talk about this."

Tidwell was so mad he came close to putting a fist through the wall.

He went back to the doorway and said, "You talk."

Janet looked awful, still sitting in the bed, hunched over amidst messy sheets and blankets. Her hair was all over the place and her face had no color. She sent the call to voicemail and tossed the phone back to the bed.

Lady was now lying on the floor in the corner with one eyebrow up.

"His name is Greg Stovall," Janet said. "We went to high school together. He found me online."

"And . . ."

Spit it out.

"We started to dialogue."

Tidwell shook his head in anger and waited, thinking that's what she'd been doing on her phone right in front of him all these weeks.

"His wife was an attorney; she was busy all the time—much like you."

"Was?" Tidwell said.

"They're divorced."

Tidwell seethed at the thought of the loser husband with blind rage.

"She was a workaholic."

"Like me," he blurted. His phone buzzed. He ignored it.

Her eyes widened and she nodded crazily. "Yes! Like you. They saw less and less of each other. They drifted apart. *Like us.* That's exactly what's happened, in case you haven't noticed!"

His nostrils flared and he said nothing.

"It's just someone to talk to, to relate to, someone who listens."

Tidwell shook his head and steamed. "I listen!"

"No. You don't! You couldn't care less about my day, my feelings. Your job consumes you. It's all you think about. When you're here, you're not here. You're not engaged with me. You're dismissive and patronizing."

"You're exaggerating and making excuses so you can do what you want—so you can have another relationship besides ours. That wasn't in our vows, Janet."

"You're an alcoholic! Okay, Dolby? It's true. You need to face it."

Behind Tidwell's laugh he was speared with emotions of hurt and guilt.

"You laugh, but it's true," she said. "You drink yourself to sleep every single night. You need help."

"Ever think you might have something to do with that?"

"Oh! It's my fault you've become a drunk."

"It's amazing how a discussion about *your affair* has turned into a list of accusations against me."

"I'm stating facts. When we got married you didn't work like this, or drink like you do."

"Janet, I'm a Sergeant with the Portland Police Bureau—"

"Ha! That's funny. You sure don't act like it."

Lady got up and left the room, unable to handle the discord.

"You don't understand what I deal with—"

"You're head of the Portland PB and you've got a depressed wife and drug-addicted son."

"When did you see this guy last?" Tidwell was determined to get it back on topic.

She shook her head and her eyes shot back and forth. "Not since our thirtieth high school reunion."

Tidwell thought back to the event. Naturally, he hadn't wanted to go because he wouldn't have known anyone. Besides, she hadn't asked him to go with her.

"Funny, you never mentioned seeing him there."

She shook her head in disgust. "Nothing happened. We talked like I talked to everyone else. Years have gone by without talking to him."

"How long have you been talking with him now?"

She pursed her lips and shook her head.

"How long?" Tidwell yelled.

"Maybe six weeks," she blurted.

That hurt.

Six weeks was a long time.

"Voice calls? Did you Facetime him or just text?"

She blinked and he instantly knew the answer.

"We Facetimed maybe three times. Some calls."

"Maybe three times. Hmm, this gets better and better."

"Oh, don't make it sound so sexual. Nothing happened when we Facetimed. We're friends."

"Of course, friends. That's how all affairs start."

"It's not an affair."

"No, but you were all set to meet up with him in person yesterday."

Her lips sealed shut and her head dropped. "For dinner. That's all."

45

"Sure, that's all. It goes from texting, to Facetiming, to dinner, to—"

"Stop!" Janet yelled, putting a hand to her head as if in pain. "After dinner I was going to Becky's." Her sister's place in Bend.

"So what was the plan, just to keep hiding this from me? Do you want a divorce or what? If I'm such a workaholic and alcoholic, maybe that's what you're wanting."

"I don't want it, Dolby, but you have to admit, we are in a bad place."

"You're dang right we are because you're having an affair. Call it what you want. The fact is you are smack dab in the middle of a relationship with another man."

Silence.

His eyes bore into her like blistering lasers.

"So, what are we going to do about all this?" Janet said.

"What do you want to do; you want to separate? Is that what you want? So you can go ahead and try someone else."

"We need help, Dolby. We need counseling."

That was the last thing he had time for or wanted to do. But she was right. They were in a very bad and scary place.

"Set it up—with someone neutral. I'll be there."

He turned and headed for another drink, but something much stronger this time.

10

DEETZ HAD thirty-five years of police experience.

He'd seen the law broken just about every which way it could be broken.

He'd seen good cops and bad cops—lazy ones, uptight ones, redneck ones, steady ones, and those who never should have been cops at all.

What he'd witnessed in the two months of partnering with Brandon amazed him at times, and Deetz was quite certain it wasn't just because Brandon was his son. The kid's reflexes were lightning fast and his intuition was keen—at times, almost uncanny. And it didn't hurt that he was a marksman medal winner.

So, when the female driver tossed the Ruger to her nasty passenger friend and he scrambled to catch it, whipped around, and raised his arm to shoot Deetz at close range, it wasn't surprising to hear—and even feel—the massive boom from Brandon's Glock. Or to see the husky passenger virtually leave the ground momentarily after the 40-caliber bullet from Brandon's gun exploded in the very center of the man's back.

The female driver screamed hysterically and settled into speechlessness.

Ambulances and squad cars arrived within nine minutes; at which time the passenger was pronounced dead at the scene. Paramedics wrapped the female driver in a mylar thermal emergency blanket at the back of the ambulance and checked her over thoroughly.

Meanwhile, Deetz and Brandon searched her vehicle and—amidst the foul garbage—found a bag of pot, three hypodermic needles, two burned-up glass pipes, and a .22 mm Browning with five bullets in the magazine.

A tall Black male paramedic approached Deetz and Brandon, rubbing his hands together. "She's been wigged out on meth for days—maybe a week. Hasn't slept much in all that time," he said. "You probably saw she's got meth mouth. Her teeth are starting to decay. She must only weigh ninety pounds and she's dehydrated. She admits she's addicted; says she wants to quit." He nodded toward the dead guy, who was being loaded onto a stretcher. "She obviously got in with the wrong crowd."

"She sure did," Deetz said. "And she acted like one of them today. We need to arrest her."

"Okay . . . but I'd feel much better if we could take her in, get her on an IV and get her fed. She's extremely weak."

"We'll let you transport her, but she's in trouble. Multiple serious charges," Deetz said. "Can we talk to her?"

The paramedic nodded and led Deetz and Brandon to where Deborah was wrapped in the foil blanket, drinking a bottle of orange Gatorade.

She glanced up at them and looked away. "Am I in trouble?"

Deetz nodded. "You are. Things weren't too bad until you tossed that gun to your friend. That made things real bad."

Deborah's head whipped toward them, then away again, and she clenched her teeth. The wind blew her greasy hair. She mumbled something.

"We're going to arrest you, but these people are going to take you to the hospital first to get you nourished," Deetz said.

Deborah huffed.

"Is that really your car?" Brandon said. "We're going to find out anyway, and you'll be better off if you tell the truth now."

"It's a friend's, okay?" she said with sudden grit.

"Where does this friend live?" Brandon said.

"I'm not telling you that—I'd be in big trouble if I did."

"You're already in big trouble," Deetz said. "You'd be smart to worry more about us than your friend right now. In fact, you can help yourself a great deal if you tell us where you got that crystal meth."

She smirked and shook her head. "I don't know anything about that. It wasn't on me. You can't charge me with that."

"Show us where the dealer is and we'll help you as much as we can," Deetz said.

Deborah gave Deetz a sour look. "I'm not telling you any more. Go ahead, arrest me. I've got no life anyway." She reached up with a trembling hand and rubbed at a raw mark beneath her eye.

"Is the person whose car you're driving the same person you got the ice from?" Brandon said.

"You're wasting your time," Deborah said. "If I narc, I'm dead, okay? Dead."

"But you understand you're going to prison as it is, right?" Deetz said. "If you give us the dealer, we can tell the judge you helped us and hopefully get you a reduced sentence."

"Believe me, if I narc on this dude—he'll get to me in prison."

If he was that powerful, Deetz wanted him even more badly.

Suddenly, Deborah's mouth and eyes dropped open wide as she fixed her gaze on something straight behind Deetz and Brandon.

Deetz heard a car approaching from behind. This was a quiet side street without another car in sight during the whole ordeal.

Deetz glanced at Brandon who was already turned around to face the approaching vehicle.

"Get down!" Brandon yelled.

Deetz caught a glimpse of a small red VW Golf buzzing toward them with a man hanging out the passenger window. He wore a dark coat and ski mask.

"Dad, get down!" Brandon shouted as he knocked Deborah to the ground.

Deetz spotted the passenger's assault rifle just before he heard it fire in rapid succession. He dove to the ground where Brandon was shielding Deborah, bashed his knee like all get out, and his glasses fell off. He scrambled to get them back on.

The shots were loud and fast.

Deetz covered Brandon and Deborah with his body and went for his gun at the same time. It crossed his mind that he was way too old for this, almost in a comical sense.

The red car slowed.

More shots split the air as if it was a war zone. The shots whizzed, pinged, and popped all around them, hitting the ambulance, the ground, and Deborah's car.

Deetz pivoted, raised his Glock to get a shot off—and his left leg exploded in pain and blood spatter. He let out a groan and rolled over in agony.

"Dad?" Brandon whipped around to see what was wrong.

The red car jerked several times as if the driver didn't know how to drive a stick shift, then took off with the engine whirring; it was too far away to see the plates.

Deetz looked around to make sure everyone was okay, then looked down at his leg.

Brandon cursed, looking at it at the same time as Deetz.

Deetz's dark navy uniform pants were torn open revealing a bloody dark hole where the bullet had entered at the side of his thigh. Blood was gushing out.

"It's okay," Deetz said out of breath, not wanting Brandon to worry. "I'm okay. We got an ambo right here. That's what I call service."

"Help!" Brandon called toward the paramedics. "Officer's been shot. Hurry!"

Deetz pressed as hard as he could with both hands against the wound, concerned about how much blood was seeping out.

"Hold it tight," Brandon said. "They'll be right here. Come on, guys!"

Brandon used his shoulder radio to call base, letting them know Deetz had been shot and giving a description of the red Golf and the direction it was headed. His voice shook. Deetz could see the concern for his old man in his son's young brown eyes.

Deetz nodded. "Don't worry. I'm good. Check the others."

Brandon stared at him and looked down at the wound. "You're losing blood bad. Give me your coat."

"Good idea." Deetz turned so Brandon could get the coat off. Brandon was afraid he would hurt Deetz if he pressed on it too hard and told his dad to do it.

Deetz grunted as he pressed the coat as hard as he could against the wound.

The same paramedic who'd treated Deborah showed up, down on both knees, moving the coat so he could look at the wound.

"Okay, keep pressing as hard as you can. I'll be right back with the stretcher."

Deetz looked at Brandon. "Go make sure everyone's okay. Then start setting up a crime scene." He was getting light-headed. "There will be casings. Tire tracks. Check for cameras."

"Dad, be quiet. Just rest. You look like you're about to pass out. I got this."

Deetz nodded and closed his eyes, thinking all he could do now was trust that God would take care of him.

"Here we go. They're here for you now. Everything's going to be fine."

With his eyes still closed, Deetz said, "They were trying to kill the girl, stop her from talking."

"I know, Dad. Please, will you just shut up?"

Deetz smiled with his eyes shut. "This ain't my first rodeo, Son."

11

LATE THAT NIGHT, after Janet had gone to bed for good, Tidwell poured another gin on the rocks with a splash of tonic and set himself up in front of his laptop in the low-lit den. As the old Pink Floyd tune went, he was comfortably numb.

Tidwell had gotten word from Sid Sikorski late that afternoon that Wayne Deetz had been shot in some kind of ambush in Edgewood but was going to be okay. Deetz and son Brandon had pulled over a suspicious car, a gun was produced, and Brandon shot and killed the passenger. Apparently, they were ambushed in an attempt on the female driver's life.

Tidwell had called Deetz earlier and, after hearing nothing, tried Joanie. She eventually called back and gave him an update on Wayne, who was in a lot of pain, but should be fine. Tidwell was going to miss that guy when the end of the year rolled around.

Meanwhile, the man Janet had been communicating with, Greg Stovall, was not difficult to find online. Quite the contrary.

Stovall was a big-wig architect based in Seattle, whose massive modern buildings were scattered across the Pacific Northwest like hotels on a Monopoly board. From sparkling glass office towers to sprawling contemporary residential complexes to colossal manufacturing plants, Greg Stovall seemed to be "the man" to turn to if a company wanted an avant-garde building in Washington, Oregon,

Idaho, British Columbia, and even into western Montana and northern California.

Not only was Stovall extremely wealthy, but he was also handsome. Longish messy blond hair, weathered tan, dimpled smile with nice teeth, and often photographed holding cigars and wearing sport jackets, loafers, and large shiny watches.

He was all over social media and must have had his Facebook, Twitter, TikTok, and Instagram accounts linked, because the exact same photos, videos, and 'stories' were displayed on each platform. He was shown snorkeling in turquoise waters, cutting ribbons at building grand openings, hiking snow-capped mountains, digging ceremonial first scoops of dirt at new project sites, playing poker on a yacht, steering a sailboat on a windy day, wearing hardhats while standing on scaffolding, and offering three-hundred-sixty-degree views of his lavish penthouse in the heart of Seattle.

Tidwell took a long pull from the sweaty glass and shook his head.

He thought of his recent embarrassing road rage incident.

He recalled with disgust the night before when the stocky paramedic accused him of smelling like booze and threatened him with the breathalyzer.

He thought of how his relationship with Janet was imploding.

He was no candidate for "God's spirit," as Deetz had put it.

Greg Stovall had looks, notoriety, success, and more money than he could spend. And he was pursuing Janet.

What if she's falling in love?

He couldn't fathom losing her.

Why wouldn't she fall for the guy?

Tidwell was washed up. He drank every single night. Not one drink or two, but in excess; more than he wanted or needed. He couldn't imagine not drinking each night—because of all the problems with Janet and the pressure of his work. He used to do other things after work, like dabble with his car, work in the garden, run out to the home improvement store, or go for walks with Janet. Now, all he could think about was making a beeline for the bar when he got home from work.

Am I an alcoholic?

He'd researched it a number of times and knew he had a

number of the symptoms: frequent hangovers; tried to stop and couldn't; had to drink more than he used to for the desired effect; caused problems in relationships; craved alcohol so badly he couldn't think of anything else.

The problem was, Tidwell loved the taste of beer and liquor, and he longed for the way it made him feel. It gave him a buzz. Took his worries away. Helped him sleep. And what about holidays and celebrations and Saturday nights? He could never give it up . . . would never want to.

He thought about what Deetz had told him about a supernatural peace and satisfaction that came from God—not the bottle. Tidwell saw that in Deetz, but Tidwell was no Wayne Deetz. In fact, he viewed himself as unfixable.

He went back to stalking Greg Stovall and noted that the man's ex-wife was in none of the photographs. Two boys—Frank and Lloyd—were captured with Stovall in several of the photos and Tidwell assumed they were his sons, named after the famous architect, Frank Lloyd Wright.

This guy is so full of himself.

Tidwell figured Janet had already looked at many of these same images herself and was probably awestruck.

What was Tidwell going to do about it?

He felt sick wondering if it may be too late.

If Janet left him, Tidwell knew deep down that his life would sink into one of darkness, ugliness, and despair. With no one there, he would probably drink himself into oblivion.

Tidwell assumed Nick did not know about his parents' troubles, or about his dad's battle with the bottle.

What a poor example I've become.

Tidwell took a hard swig of gin, savored the taste, and entered his name and password into the Portland Police Bureau's internal website. From there, he logged into Oregon's police database, LEDS —the Law Enforcement Data Systems. Since virtually everyone had bones in their closets, Tidwell would run Greg Stovall's name through the system and find out what dirt the big architect had that Janet didn't know about yet. Tidwell would love more than anything to be able to surprise Janet with the news that the big-time business mogul she was falling in love with had a thing for prostitutes, or had a record for larceny, assault, fraud—anything.

Several minutes later, Tidwell sat staring at the screen, stunned.

Greg Stovall was as clean as a new car just off the assembly line. He had no record, no priors, no disputes with the law, whatsoever. Tidwell couldn't find so much as a traffic ticket.

How can that be? Everyone has something to hide.

Tidwell finished his drink and continued to research Stovall's name on the internet. As the minutes ticked past, the man became more and more enviable. He was ranked among the top five-hundred philanthropists in the country, having given millions of dollars to research on cancer and Parkinson's disease, as well as toward autism in children.

Janet will love that.

His wife had a big heart and often wanted to give to various organizations. Sometimes Tidwell agreed, somewhat begrudgingly, but often he would manage to change the subject and squelch Janet's generous intentions.

His spiral into the abyss was all playing out before him now.

He looked at the empty glass.

Could it be that bad? Could booze change me that much?

Without alcohol, maybe he'd get his energy and zeal back. Maybe he'd feel clean and alive when he woke up in the mornings. Maybe he'd begin to live again in the evenings—get out, go places, work with his hands, give Janet the attention she needed. It would be good for his liver and his overall health. He could lose weight. Perhaps he could even help Nick get through his trials, rather than drowning his own sorrows every night and basically ignoring his son's issues.

Lady wandered into the den and laid down in her usual spot right up against the leather ottoman. She looked at Tidwell, smiling with her mouth open and big eyes shining. Sometimes, he felt the dog was trying to tell him something, or to help in some way.

Tidwell reached for his phone, opened to his text messages, and scrolled until he found the one from Wayne's son's girlfriend, Tammy, the social worker. He scanned the message until he found the name of the addiction recovery group she'd mentioned for Nick:

The Morning 7s. He put the phone down and searched the group on his laptop.

The Morning 7s met in Wicker and dealt with everything from PTSD to drug addiction and alcoholism. The more Tidwell read about it, the more convinced he was The Morning 7s wasn't for him.

Next, he searched Alcoholics Anonymous and found a group that met early each morning at a Presbyterian church about halfway between the house and the police bureau. He read about what to expect at the meetings. He read that they studied what they called the Big Book and relied on a Higher Power. He could try it, but he was concerned about his anonymity. If anyone found out he was a local police sergeant, he could be fired.

Tidwell closed the laptop and sat in silence.

He thought about Wayne Deetz—how upbeat he'd been when Tidwell talked to him on the phone that afternoon from the hospital. Ever since Deetz had begun going to church several years ago at the invitation of J.P. and Tammy, he'd become a new man. Tidwell had witnessed the transformation. He never said much to Deetz about it, but he'd watched admirably and even waited to see if the change would last. To Tidwell's amazement, not only had it lasted, but Deetz's character, his personality, had become even more enviable over time. He had a peace and joy about him—a steadiness and a care for others—that intrigued Tidwell.

Tidwell arose from his chair with a grunt, snatched his glass, and went into the kitchen with Lady in tow. The house was silent. He put several ice cubes in his glass, retrieved the bottle of gin from the cupboard, filled the glass, added a splash of tonic, stirred it with a finger, and took a drink.

Ahh.

This may be his last for a while.

He owed it to Janet and Nick—and to himself—to get sober, to see if that would make a difference in their messed-up lives.

That process would begin tomorrow.

But for now, Tidwell would drink, and he would drink heartily.

"Cheers, Lady," he whispered.

12

BRANDON AND KRISTEN sat at the kitchen table in Brandon's apartment late that Friday night with huge bowls of mint chocolate chip ice cream in front of them. Brandon's roommate, Clarence, was several feet away in the kitchen cooking an omelet in the biggest pan they owned.

"You dodged one today, Buddy," Clarence said as he sprinkled a huge handful of shredded cheese into the pan. "I bet your mom was worried sick about your dad."

"Actually, I was shocked how well she took it. It was a clean wound. The surgery was fast. He's going to be fine. And she knows he's done in a few months so she's seeing the light at the end of the tunnel."

"Leena was the one who was stressed," Kristen said.

"She and my dad are so tight," Brandon said. "She was really worried while he was in surgery."

"She was pacing around in his room having a conversation with Jesus while he was in there." Kristen laughed. "It was so cute. That girl is something . . . And when he got back to the room—oh my gosh, she was so relieved. She is so sensitive. Just precious."

"So, he's home though, right?" Clarence said.

"Yeah," Brandon said. "He hurt the knee on the same leg that got shot, so he's pretty banged up. He'll be on crutches. But I think it dawned on us after his surgery how lucky we were."

"I'll say," Clarence said.

"Wayne was actually in a really good mood," Kristen said. "He wasn't complaining at all. He was more interested in what Brandon found at the crime scene than anything else."

"That red Golf shouldn't be hard to find," Clarence said.

"You wouldn't think so, but we haven't so far," Brandon said.

"What about the casings?" Clarence said.

"Ballistics said it was a compact AR, like a little sub-machine gun. Inexpensive. You should have heard it, the shots sounded hollow. They're trying to zero in on a make and model. But he fired at least twenty-three rounds."

Kristen scowled and glared at Brandon, who realized he hadn't told her that yet.

Uh oh. She's going to be upset.

"That girl must know something important if they came after her like that," Clarence said.

"I know," Brandon said.

"She's in the hospital?" Clarence said.

"Was. They had her on an IV for a few hours and then we booked her. She's in lockup until she goes before a judge tomorrow."

"You think they'll set bail for her?" Clarence said.

"Probably. Who knows if anyone will pay to get her out though."

"You need to be watching that," Clarence said.

Kristen looked into Brandon's eyes extra-long as she took a spoonful of ice cream.

"What?" Brandon said to her.

Her eyes rose and fell. "Nothing. I just worry about you."

"Ha, ha," Clarence roared as he plated his omelet and came over to join them at the table. "Get used to that, little lady. You need to talk to Joanie about that. Thirty-five years of being married to a Portland cop. Not for the faint of heart."

Brandon silently reflected on the cold fact that he had shot and killed two men during his first two months on the job. In a quiet moment they'd shared after his dad's surgery that afternoon, Deetz had assured Brandon how unusual that was. Deetz told him that in his thirty-five years of police work he'd only shot four people, none of whom had died.

"In all that time, Dad never killed anyone," Brandon said.

Clarence laughed. "And you've killed two in two months!"

"It's not funny," Brandon said, glancing at Kristen. "Wait till it happens to you," he said to Clarence. "It'll keep you up at night, that's for sure."

The guilt was something Brandon had discussed with the police therapist, Dr. Terri Wallender, who had assured him he was in the right, protecting the innocent, good versus evil, and all that.

But still, taking a person's life as Brandon had done that day—it was not only a harrowing experience, but an inexplicable, other-worldly one. Both shootings were seared in his mind with high-definition clarity.

Brandon felt Kristen's hand cover his.

"Hopefully, you'll never have to do it again," Kristen said softly.

"Amen to that," Clarence said. "Hopefully neither of us will."

THE JULY NIGHT had cooled considerably by the time Brandon walked Kristen to his car to drive her home.

"Look at that moon," he said.

"And the stars," she said. "So beautiful."

He opened her door for her, looked into her eyes, and kissed her. They both smiled. Her bright eyes sparkled.

"Well, thank you," she said. "What was that for?"

"For hanging out with me and being such a great friend."

"Ha! Friend? Is that all we are after seven weeks?"

"I didn't realize we were counting."

"We most certainly are!"

They got in and headed toward the house where Kristen rented a room with four other people, each of whom had their own room. She wore a loose white short-sleeved shirt with a swoop neck, which revealed the small tattoo in script letters at the base of the back of her neck: *S U R V I V O R*.

"So, you're saying those guys took at least twenty-three shots at you and your dad today?" she said.

He'd known this would be coming ever since he'd opened his big mouth to Clarence.

"Well, technically they were aiming for the girl we were arresting."

"Brandon, I'm not a wimp. You know that by now. I can handle just about anything." She reached over and took his hand. "You mean so much to me. I couldn't handle it if anything happened to you."

He glanced over at her. She was staring at him, her brown eyes rimmed with tears.

"Hey, don't do that," he said. "I'm here. I'm fine. I'm always going to be fine."

"You don't know that. You're fine now, but what about tomorrow and every day after that?"

What is she trying to say?

Brandon shook his head. "It's my job, Kris. That's what it is. Sometimes it's dangerous. Most of the time it's not."

She sniffed. "I just . . . I've never had this . . . what we have. It's like a dream. I never thought I'd meet anyone like you."

Brandon couldn't believe her words. Was she trying to tell him that she loved him? He was almost certain he felt the same about her, but this was heavy. And happening fast.

"I'm enjoying what we have," he said. "Let's just keep taking it a day at a time."

The silence that followed made Brandon feel as if he had hurt her feelings. But what he'd said was what he thought was best; he didn't regret it.

They arrived in Kristen's neighborhood and Brandon pulled his car up in front of the house and parked.

"What's your day look like tomorrow?" he said, attempting to end the evening on a positive note.

"I told you that already," Kristen snapped. "I work eight to four. You weren't listening."

Brandon stared at her.

"What are you mad about?" he said.

"Three times during this drive you've implied that our relationship is just a casual friendship."

"What?" he squawked.

"Calling me a 'great friend.' Acting like you don't care we've been dating seven weeks. Saying 'let's just take it a day at a time.'"

"Kristen, I've loved the last seven weeks. It's been great. We've had a wonderful time together. All I said was, let's keep it going and see what happens. That's positive!"

"In other words, no commitment," she said.

"You don't see me dating anyone else, do you?"

"Not until someone better comes along."

This is downright weird. What is happening?

"Okay, look, I'm wiped out," Brandon said. "I don't think we should have this conversation now. Let's both get some sleep and we can—"

"Fine." Kristen threw her door open, got out, slammed the door, and headed up the driveway.

Brandon got out. "Hey, wait," he called. "Come back here, Kris. We're not done."

"I'm done," she called, without looking back.

13

THE BEDROOM WAS DARK.

Tidwell's head felt like an enormous lead balloon.

He had a feeling the alarm clock radio had been playing for quite some time before he'd heard it.

He remembered he'd promised himself to go to that AA meeting.

He reached over with a groan, hit the sleep switch, and closed his eyes.

His head pounded so hard he could hear it thump every three seconds.

He opened his eyes and stared at Janet's dresser to stop the spinning. When that didn't work, he threw his right leg out from under the sheets and set his size thirteen foot on the floor to steady the ship.

His mouth was dry as a towel.

After lying there in agony a few more minutes, he sat up.

He swayed and rubbed his eyes.

Sadly, this was nothing new for the reputable police sergeant.

He considered skipping the AA meeting, re-setting the alarm, and going back to sleep. But his rocky status with Janet and her interest in the handsome Greg Stovall ran through his mind—as did his troubled son Nick.

I've got to try this.

Tidwell sighed, stood with a grunt, and padded into the bath-room, slightly off balance.

His feet hurt and he vowed to lose weight as he did every morn-ing. Even though he was six-foot-three, he was still thirty pounds over what he should weigh.

He stood at the sink in his black boxers and drank three full glasses of water. He leaned closer to the mirror. His eyes were small and bloodshot. His face was . . . old.

He didn't want to look at himself.

He wanted to change. *Needed* to change.

He headed for the shower, wondering how differently he would feel in the mornings if he were sober.

TIDWELL SAT in his Charger in the church parking lot, waiting until the last minute before going into the AA meeting. He was nervous and that wasn't like him. Janet had been asleep when he'd left. He'd thrown on jeans and a plain gray T-shirt and sandals for the meeting. His uniform was in a duffle bag in the back seat; he would change when he got to work.

Seven or eight cars dotted the parking lot, everything from a new Tesla to a vintage Ford pickup truck that leaned to one side.

At two minutes before meeting time, Tidwell walked across the parking lot with the sun just beginning to silhouette the sprawling church building. He headed for the only light on inside. The large wooden door was propped open a few inches with a piece of wood. He went inside and saw a sign with AA and an arrow pointing down the hallway.

It was quiet.

He followed the smell of coffee and the light coming from a room down the hallway, which looked extremely bright. He got to the doorway, stopped, and sized up the situation.

Three men and two women sat in chairs in the shape of a circle about ten feet wide. Another man poured himself a Styrofoam cup of coffee at a table at the end of the room. Above the table was a whiteboard with words in black marker that read: "Welcome to AA. It's going to be a GREAT day."

Tidwell acknowledged those seated and went for the coffee pot.

The room was very tranquil and only a few of the people in the circle spoke in quiet voices he couldn't understand.

The man leaving the coffee pot had brown hair combed over. He wore big glasses and looked to be about thirty-five. "Morning," he said quietly to Tidwell as they passed each other.

"Morning," Tidwell said. He didn't want to keep the group waiting, but he could really use coffee. He quickly grabbed a cup and took the carafe and poured. Both hands trembled. He forced himself to take a deep breath, exhaled, turned around, and approached the circle.

There was just enough space between chairs to squeeze through. He sat in a squeaky chair with an empty chair to his left and a man with a black beard to his right. The man had calloused, worker hands and a dark brown corduroy coat that smelled awfully of cigarettes.

"We'll wait another minute before we start," said a white-haired man across the circle. He had bright eyes, a sharp jaw, clean skin, and reading glasses. He was thin and wore baggy jeans and running shoes. Tidwell guessed him to be close to seventy and perhaps the leader of the band.

A pretty woman across the circle with a pointy nose and dark eyebrows spoke in a low tone to the man next to her. He wore dark gray slacks and a matching jacket, white shirt, no tie, shiny black shoes. They were discussing an upcoming concert and how the venue was now charging thirty dollars for parking. The well-dressed man and his wife were planning to Uber while the pretty woman said she and her sister would pay whatever it cost to park and to have the chance to see the artist, whomever it was.

"Let's get started," said the gray-haired man. "I hope you're all well. For any first-timers, this is Alcoholics Anonymous, a fellowship of men and women who share experiences, strength, and hope with each other so we may solve our common problem and help others recover from alcoholism. The only requirement for membership is a desire to stop drinking. There are no dues or membership fees."

The man had this memorized and said it from the heart.

"Our primary purpose is to stay sober and to help other alcoholics achieve sobriety."

The gritty-looking woman to Tidwell's left, just past the empty chair, whispered those last words with her eyes closed as the gray-haired man said them.

"My name is Elmore, and I'm an alcoholic," said the gray-haired man. "For those of you who don't know, we take turns facilitating the meetings on a month-to-month basis. July is my month. Today I'd like to start us off by reading a poem I found written on a card that was buried in a library book I was reading. It says it's by a man named Walter Smith. I couldn't find any more than that about the man."

Elmore paused, cleared his throat, adjusted his reading glasses, and began to read from a small card he held out in front of him.

"The search is over—the journey's been long.
But now I know where I truly belong.
For I came to a fork in the road of life,
one headed toward peace, one headed toward strife.
By the grace of God, I chose the right way.
And that, my dear friends, keeps me sober today."

Elmore smiled with a frown, sniffed, and fought to harness his emotions. He paused for a good ten seconds. Tidwell was touched by it and felt that he himself was at a fork in the road, with one lane leading to peace and another toward strife.

Elmore huffed and continued.

"He's given me hope and the will to be strong—
with understanding and love He's forgiven each wrong.
I'm indebted to Him for leading the way,
as I know in my heart He gave me AA.
AA is my home, my salvation, my peace—
I pray that my faith shalt ever increase."

Elmore looked up, looked at the faces around the circle, and said the last part by heart.

"For the 'sickness' we share is not a sin nor a crime,

and our problems we'll solve—one day at a time."

Everyone around the circle snapped their fingers and murmured their approval. A tear streaked down the face of the attractive woman across the circle. Tidwell nodded and kept back his emotions.

"Who'd like to share what's going on?" Elmore said.

Tidwell looked down at his big, clasped hands, certain he wasn't going to say anything—and hoping to God they weren't going to ask him to speak.

I'm not saying a word.

"Well, let's just say I had a heck of a day yesterday," said the gritty lady of about sixty. She had blondish graying hair, tanning booth skin that was extremely wrinkled beneath her eyes and around the base of her neck. She had a gravelly smoker's voice.

"You guys know me." She glanced at Tidwell. "Well, you don't. I'm Beverly and I'm an alcoholic. I'm an administrative assistant in the used car business. Anyway, there was a party last night at my boss's house. I did not want to go because I knew the temptation would be strong, but he's my boss so I had to go. Anyway, the booze was flowing like you wouldn't believe. Open bar. Whatever you wanted, all you wanted. No one watching."

Several of the people around the circle nodded and mumbled sympathetically.

"Usually, I'm okay at parties, well, that is, since I've been coming here for the last year. But last night I got really mad. Because I wanted a drink. Why can everyone else have a good time and I can't? It just ticked me off so bad."

Tidwell looked to her left and the man seated next to her was now staring directly at Tidwell—and he looked vaguely familiar. Forties. Dark curly hair. Black glasses. A bit of a bulging stomach. Casually dressed.

Could be anyone.

As the man continued to stare, Tidwell's face warmed with embarrassment. He looked down for quite a few seconds, looked back up, and the guy was still staring at him with a dark eyebrow raised.

Tidwell couldn't place the man but he was almost certain his face looked familiar. He wondered if the man recognized him as a sergeant with the Portland Police Bureau.

While Beverly continued explaining how she practically ran outside at the party to smoke and call her AA sponsor, Tidwell shuffled through the options of who this guy could be—a reporter, a colleague, a former criminal?

"Needless to say," Beverly continued, "today I'm proud I stood my ground. Thrilled. You know that feeling? I overcame. It could have been a totally different story, and if it had, if I had given in to the urge to drink, I'd be so depressed right now."

"Good for you," said the man in the suit.

While everyone nodded and agreed and congratulated her, the man who'd been staring at Tidwell—and was still looking at him with a weird smirk on his face—smiled and very briefly pointed his index finger at Tidwell in the shape of a gun and pulled the trigger.

14

THE SECOND DEETZ realized he was awake, his left leg felt as if it was on fire. Then he realized his entire body screamed with pain, as if it had been crushed in a trash compactor.

Joanie was gone from the bed and had shut the door—off to make coffee and have her quiet time.

Deetz tried not to move because each movement delivered intense pain.

It's worse because I'm so old.

He was usually awake before Joanie, at 5:30, to run or work out, but he'd decided to sleep in one day to recoup from the shooting.

One day . . . what a laugh!

The way he felt now, he wouldn't be working out again for months.

He heard footsteps. The door opened quietly and Joanie peeked in.

"Thank God," he said. "Could you get me the pain meds, honey?"

Joanie came in wearing her white robe and moccasins with her arms crossed. "Is it bad?"

Deetz nodded. "Not only the leg. Everywhere."

"You poor thing. Hold on." She shuffled into the bathroom and came back with a white pill and a glass of water. "I worry about you taking these. They're super strong." She meant because synthetic opioids could be addictive but right now, Deetz didn't care—he had to take something to relieve the pain.

"Don't worry." He grimaced as he sat up enough to drink. "I really need it." Joanie fluffed his pillows. Deetz took the pill, drank, and eased back down onto the pillows.

"Can you sleep more?" she said.

"I hope so, but I doubt it."

She sat on the edge of the bed and ran a soft hand over his balding head.

"This is going to take time," she said.

It was dawning on him how true that was.

He sighed and closed his eyes. "That girl goes before the judge today. Have you heard anything from Brandon?"

"Wayne, will you please forget about that and go to sleep? My gosh. For once in your life can you just rest and take care of yourself? That's an order. You sleep. I'll have something for you to eat when you wake up. What do you want?"

The base of his throat felt nauseous.

"Nothing sounds good," he said.

"Maybe an egg. I'll check with you in a bit."

She leaned over and kissed his forehead. "I love you. I'm going to take good care of you."

"Love you," he said softly.

She went for the door quietly and Leena entered. "Hey, Dad."

She came over to the bed and Deetz tried to act like he wasn't dying. "Hi, honey."

"Wow, you have looked better," she said, staring down at him. "Mom said not to touch you."

He nodded and smiled. "I'm going to be okay."

"Not many girls can say their dads got shot." Leena began hobbling around on Deetz's crutches. "I was worried about you during the surgery."

"Let's let Dad get some more rest," Joanie said, standing at the door.

Leena leaned the crutches back where they had been and knelt down by the bed. "I think we should pray."

"Okay," Deetz said, welcoming her simple faith.

"Dear Jesus, please heal Dad really fast. Take away the pain. Help him be comfortable. Don't let him become a drug addict; we don't need that. Please protect Brandon and help him keep his head on a swivel. Amen."

Joanie had obviously told Leena about the dangers of opioids. Deetz had to laugh to himself. Those two, when they were alone, were like a couple of old ladies.

Leena's faith always stopped Deetz in his tracks. She was so relational. She just seemed to walk with God all day long, conversing with him like an invisible friend. Even when she'd been kidnapped a year earlier at the age of eighteen, her faith seemed bulletproof, she'd gone through the terror unscathed.

"Okay, Pops. We'll check on you later." Leena headed out the door with Joanie.

Silence.

As the medication worked its way through Deetz's bloodstream subtly beginning to mask the pain, he closed his eyes, forced himself to relax, and thanked God for protecting him and Brandon.

He was so tired.

He wondered if the driver of the car from yesterday, Deborah, would get out on bail—and what would happen to her if she did.

He wondered if Nick Tidwell had sought help for his addiction.

He wondered what Tidwell had been about to tell him at the hospital that night—about what Janet had been up to.

He nodded off for a moment then opened his eyes and stared out the window.

Deetz was sixty now.

Sixty.

The majority of his life had been lived. How much did he and Joanie have left—twenty years? Less? And how many of those would be healthy, enjoyable years?

One thing he knew for sure, he was too old for police work anymore.

He had just six more months until retirement and full pension.

He was dropping into a peaceful sleep.

Please . . . keep Joanie and me healthy to enjoy the next chapter.

He thought of J.P. and Tammy and the prospect of having grand-children someday.

He wondered what the future held for Brandon and his girl-friend. Then Tidwell crept back into his mind and Deetz was over-come with a feeling of restlessness. Now, more than ever, Deetz needed to be a friend to the guy. He vowed to do so as he drifted off to sleep.

15

TIDWELL'S first AA meeting was almost over and the hour had flown past because he'd been absorbed by what the people had to say—and somewhat relieved. The man who'd stared him down earlier said at one point that his name was Neil and that in his worst drinking days he would consume two to three bottles of cheap whiskey per day. *Per day!*

Tidwell drank nowhere near that much and by the time they were finished with the moment of silence Elmore had asked for, Tidwell was convinced he was not an alcoholic.

"Just a reminder," Elmore said, "next to the coffee station there are copies of the Big Book and of the AA devotional, which are free of charge. Take one if you like. If it's your first day of sobriety be sure to take a white chip indicating that you are surrendering, that you are giving up your old way of living. If you need a sponsor, get with me after the meeting or call me, my number is up on the whiteboard, and I will connect you with a sponsor."

As everyone stood Tidwell thought, *Okay, good, I can check this off my list.*

"One last thing before we go," Elmore said, as he passed sheets of white paper around the circle. "Let's stand together, just stand behind your chairs, and let's read aloud The 12 Steps together."

Oh, brother.

Tidwell almost darted out, but they'd begun reading before he could move.

"Number one," Elmore led them, "we admitted we were power-less over alcohol—that our lives had become unmanageable."

Tidwell didn't read aloud but did focus on the words that jumped out at him: 'powerless' and 'unmanageable.'

"Two," Elmore and the others continued, "we came to believe that a Power greater than ourselves could restore us to sanity. Three, we made a decision to turn our will and our lives over to the care of God . . ."

Tidwell was antsy. It was as if God himself was prodding him to get off the fencepost and believe in him or to make some kind of commitment to him.

But Tidwell loved his beer and his liquor, and he couldn't see that ever changing. Besides, his drinking was nothing compared with these people. In a way, he was relieved.

To those in the room, alcohol was a dirty word because it was an obsession that consumed and ravaged their lives every waking minute, causing chaos, mayhem, and havoc. They couldn't take a drink like he could, and not have ten drinks. Alcohol was their Achilles' heel.

They finished reading the twelfth step and the meeting adjourned. It crossed Tidwell's mind to grab a cup of coffee for the road, but he did not want to be forced to speak to anyone, so he turned and headed out the door without looking back.

He heard footsteps in the hallway behind him moving quickly so he took longer strides and pushed the large wooden door open to the outside and headed for his car.

The door squeaked open behind him.

"Hey, wait up," came a man's voice.

Tidwell kept going straight toward the Charger.

"Hey, hold up!"

When Tidwell was twenty-five feet from his car he unlocked it with his remote and turned around to see if the voice was calling him.

It was the man who'd stared at him so weirdly in the meeting and had pointed at him, as if with a gun. He now gave a wave and hurried toward Tidwell.

Oh, brother.

"Your first time, right?" The man was about five-foot-eight and wide-bodied. He was out of breath and put on a navy windbreaker as he waited for Tidwell to respond.

"Yeah," Tidwell said, continuing toward his car.

"What'd you think?" the man called, continuing his approach.

Tidwell turned back as he walked, "Really good," he said. "Take care."

The man was still heading toward him across the parking lot.

"Will you come back?" the man said.

Tidwell got to his car and looked back at the man. "Probably not, but it was really good. Good luck to you." He started to get in.

"You don't recognize me, do you?" the man approached Tidwell's car.

Tidwell straightened, turned, and stared at the man, waiting for the big punchline.

"Why aren't you coming back? Don't think you have a problem?" the man said.

Whoa.

Tidwell tilted his head and glared at the guy, his temperature rising.

"I never forget a face—or a car," the man nodded toward Tidwell's Charger.

Again, Tidwell tried to remember where he'd seen the guy's wide face and thick neck, but when he couldn't he decided to just leave. He got in the car and started to shut the door.

"Road rage!" the man yelled.

Something clicked in Tidwell's memory bank and he sat there staring at the guy with his door open, feeling as if he was drilled to the seat.

"Remember?" the guy said, pointing to a dark car across the parking lot. He held one of the little black devotional books in his hand. "That's my Beamer over there. You remember running me off the road a couple days ago, over at that busy intersection at Kennedy?"

Tidwell groaned inside, shook his head, and lied, "What are you talking about?"

The man laughed nervously and ruffled his curly hair.

"That's what this disease is all about, man: denial."

With that word, 'denial,' Tidwell felt as if he'd been blasted with a double-barrel shotgun.

The wind left him.

He just sat there staring at the little guy, contemplating whether he could be some kind of angel or something.

"I know you remember," the man said, and tossed the little book into Tidwell's lap. "That kind of rage isn't normal. You had a gun on you! What are you doing here, anyway? Why'd you come if you don't think you have a drinking problem?"

"Man," Tidwell dropped his head, looked at the small book, and sighed, "you have seriously got me mistaken for somebody else. But I appreciate what you're trying to do."

"I'm trying to help you. I see your car! I recognized you the second you came in that room because you're like eight feet tall."

Tidwell hit the ignition and the car rumbled to life. He looked at the guy but had no words. He was panicked. He just wanted to get out of there before someone discovered that he worked for the PPB.

"So you're just going to drive off and try to forget this," the man shook his head. "I'm trying to help you. I'll be your sponsor if you want. I just lost mine."

Tidwell gave a chuckle to hide his guilt. He pushed the gas and the car revved.

"You pulled a gun on me, dude."

Once again, his words hit Tidwell like a shot.

"That is not normal, man. I can help you." The man threw his arms back toward the church. "*We* can help you. Just come back. That's all you have to do. One day at a time."

"Dude, I appreciate what you're trying to do, but you're mistaken. That was not me. And, unlike the rest of you, I am not an alcoholic."

Tidwell slammed his door to shut off the drama and goosed the Charger through the parking lot to the exit, not looking back, not wanting to remember any of it.

16

BRANDON HAD BEEN restless all night and had gotten very little sleep after Kristen's weird behavior the night before. To make matters worse, when he reported to work the next morning, he was told his partner and "mentor" for the day would be none other than Harold Rickert—the leathery old veteran who was normally Clarence's partner. Clarence had the day off and Rickert had apparently requested overtime.

"How's the old man?" Rickert said as Brandon drove the Interceptor down Fremont Avenue toward the area of his and his dad's normal beat.

"He's in a lot of pain," Brandon said, a bit nervous to be under Rickert's microscope. "My mom said he was awake through the night."

"Ah, he's a tough old bird. He'll be fine," Rickert said nonchalantly as he stared out the passenger window. "He doesn't have much time left, does he?"

"End of the year he hangs it up," Brandon said.

"Is that thirty-five?" Rickert said.

"Yes, sir. He had a couple years recently where he thought he might hang it up early. But he'll get full pension starting in December or January."

"He'd have been an idiot not to stick it out," said Rickert, who smelled like cheap aftershave and wore no jacket. His tan, hairy wrists were the size of bread loaves. "Hell, I'm gonna work as long as I can. Don't know what I'd do with myself if I ever retired. Course, I'm not married anymore."

Brandon drove in silence, his mind clouded as he tried to replay all that had gone down with Kristen the night before.

Rickert produced a can of snuff the size of a hockey puck, removed the lid, pinched a glob, and stuffed it in his lower lip. The remnant left on his fingers he snorted into his nose.

"You've been a busy boy," Rickert said, putting the tin back in his pocket. "First you kill the shooter at the coffee company your first day on the job, and yesterday you drop a gangbanger in Edgewood. Pretty impressive."

Brandon wasn't proud of killing anyone and wasn't sure how to respond. "Well," he finally said shyly. "They were both . . . out of necessity."

Rickert laughed and waved a hand. "You don't have to explain to me, kid. You've got to do what you did—every single time, without hesitation. They're the bad guys, we're the good guys. That's what I keep telling your roommate, Waters. I drill it into his head every day. If you or your partner are in danger, *do not hesitate*; shoot first, ask questions later."

Brandon contemplated Rickert's words, then wondered what had really happened the night Rickert's partner, Lance Burke, was murdered by a shot to the neck. Had Rickert hesitated in some way, or had Officer Burke? Was Rickert covering up something? Why did Rickert's ear look like it had been bitten the next day?

"Just believe me when I say, hesitation kills good cops. I take that back, hesitation kills cops; if they were good cops, they wouldn't hesitate." He laughed at his own joke. "But seriously, don't ever forget that. It's my pet peeve. These politically correct nutcases want us to baby these thugs, give them every opportunity to overtake us, or get away. It makes me sick. They have no idea what we're up against out here. You'd think we were the criminals."

They rode in silence for a moment and Brandon chuckled to himself about how raw Rickert was, and how glad he was Rickert wasn't his full-time partner.

"When I tell you to get out of the car, you get out of the car!" Rickert yelled, as if talking to a real criminal who refused his command. "I'm the law, you're the citizen! If you've done nothing wrong, everything will be fine. In the meantime, do what I say, when I say so! What is so wrong with that? That is how the law *must* work. But no, everything we do now has got to be done with such *gentleness* and *sensitivity*." He pronounced those last words with a syrupy feminine accent. "And why? Because we would never want to offend anyone because of their color or gender, even if they are spit-in-your-face reprobates. Makes me sick. It's just downright lawlessness is what it is."

Rickert had worked himself into a lather and Brandon decided to play along to learn more about the man.

"So did something specific happen on the job to make you so adamant about that—about not hesitating?" Brandon said cautiously.

Rickert's head turned, he stared at Brandon.

Brandon glanced at him and looked back at the road, questioning whether he should have been so bold.

"I've killed four people, seriously wounded eleven, and paralyzed one for life." Rickert spit into a Styrofoam cup, with some dripping down his chin. "In each case, if I hadn't shot first, I'd be dead now—and some low-life scum would be alive instead of me. No, nothing happened specifically. But I have seen cops get killed or wounded because they hesitated. It will *never* happen to me. And you should never let it happen to you."

"What happened that night with your partner, Lance Burke?" Brandon said.

"Why are you asking me about that?" Rickert blurted, with a big vein protruding from his forehead. "Waters asked me the same thing. What is it with you guys?"

"Oh, no reason," Brandon back peddled, uneasy because he had hit a nerve with Rickert. "I guess I just wondered if Burke died because he hesitated. I don't know the details."

That wasn't completely true. He knew what his dad had told him.

"There was no hesitation that night. We were blindsided." Rickert's voice was deep and clear. "Burke got shot from the shadows. The gang scattered. Burke was bleeding out so he was my first priority."

Rickert spit in the cup again and stared out his window.

"Was Burke married?" Brandon said.

"Yep. Little boy and girl. And those lazy little cowards . . . they took his life—for nothing. For something to do."

"Burke and Tidwell were best friends, I hear," Brandon said.

"I don't want to talk about it anymore," Rickert said.

Brandon's phone buzzed. He got it out and looked at the screen. It was his mom. He thought he'd better take it because it might be about Deetz. He answered the call to his ear, purposefully not trying not to sound like a mama's boy in front of Rickert.

"Hi Son."

"Hey Mom. Dad okay?"

"Okay. Not great. But the reason I'm calling is because . . . Kristen's here."

What?

"What's she doing there?" Brandon said, completely dumbfounded.

"Well, she says she wants to see Dad . . . see how he's doing."

Brandon could tell by the tone of Joanie's voice that she thought it was extremely awkward.

Kristen barely knew them. She certainly didn't know them well enough to show up unannounced with Dad seriously injured and hobbling around in his pajamas.

"Where is she now?" Brandon said, his face burning with embarrassment.

"Sitting in the living room. I told Dad she was here and, well, you know your dad. He's so nice . . . he's splashing some water on his face and said he'd see her."

"That's ridiculous," Brandon said, shooting a glance at Rickert. "She didn't tell me she was doing this. I'm going to call her, Mom."

He thought another moment.

"Just tell her he's not up for visitors," Brandon said.

"Too late," Joanie said. "Dad's getting ready and she's waiting. I just thought, well, you should know." Joanie chuckled. "It does seem a bit odd just because we don't know her that well and Dad's about a one out of ten right now."

"Right. I'm calling her, Mom. Sorry about this. I'll be in touch."

Brandon was mad. He looked at Rickert and told him he had to take care of something really quickly. Rickert just waved that it was okay and was probably loving every minute of the drama.

Brandon realized he couldn't talk in front of Rickert. He pulled the Interceptor into a Safeway parking lot, threw it in park, and told Rickert he would be right back.

Once out of the car, Brandon dialed Kristen.

To his astonishment, Rickert got out of the SUV and stood by his door, stretching his arms and legs.

Brandon walked further out of earshot, but Kristen wasn't answering her phone; it went to voicemail, which really ticked him off.

What is she doing?

He texted her:

Hey. My dad really isn't up for visitors. Call me.

Brandon paced.

Rickert was now leaning against the Interceptor with both arms resting above the passenger window, cup in one hand.

She better call.

Brandon couldn't wait much longer. It wouldn't look good to keep Rickert waiting, plus they had a job to do.

His phone vibrated.

He looked at the screen.

Her text read:

Too late!

And there was a photo attachment.

He opened it.

It was a selfie of Kristen smiling with her mouth and eyes wide open, leaning down next to a disheveled Deetz, whose pale face was peppered with gray beard stubble, whose glasses were crooked, and whose expression was one of utter confusion.

17

THE RUN-IN with the little man, Neil Houser, rattled Tidwell badly. Without making a conscientious decision to do so, he ended up at The Leprechaun bottle shop on his way into the Portland Police Bureau. It was a small, one-story, tacky looking joint with a green metal roof, grimy windows, and white neon lights stating it was open twenty-four hours.

Tidwell hadn't lied to Wayne Deetz when he'd told him he hadn't been drinking during the day. So how ridiculous was it that Tidwell chose now to start, right after leaving his first AA meeting.

Something about the confrontation with Neil Houser had set Tidwell back. Plus the fact that Janet was basically cheating on him. And the problems with Nick. It all added up to—Tidwell needed a drink. He needed to feel how only alcohol could make him feel.

A lot of good the AA meeting did.

He got back to the Charger carrying a brown bag that contained a fifth of Beefeater gin, a pack of gum, and a pack of mints. His heart pounded rapidly in anticipation of tasting the liquor. He went to set the bag in the passenger seat and saw the small devotional book Neil had tossed to him in the church parking lot.

He picked up the small black hardbound book, which was not much larger than a deck of cards. He opened it to the inside front cover. It was signed "Neil Houser" with his phone number written in black marker.

Tidwell didn't know much about AA, but he knew many of the members had what they called 'sponsors,' friends and fellow AA members they could call when they were tempted to drink, kind of like a buddy system.

Tidwell fanned through the pages of the small book and eyed the bag of gin. He realized he didn't have a cup in the car and was going to have to drink straight out of the bottle, which was not cool.

What the heck are you doing? This is not you.

He found the day's date in the little book and began reading: "We who are alcoholics begin making progress toward the good life, the clean life, the joy-filled life when we realize *we are not* the center of the universe. This life is not all about us! It is when we get our eyes off ourselves that we get a grip on the true meaning of life. It is when we surrender our lives to God that we experience true power and self-control and peace."

Tidwell kept his thumb on the page, closed the book in his lap, sighed, and shook his head. Somehow, he knew there was truth in the words he'd just read, but the allure of the liquor was commanding and, frankly, offered many more rewards. He wanted to taste the gin and he wanted its effects—it would take the stress away, help him cope with all the problems, and give him a sense of euphoria.

Tidwell tossed the book into the passenger seat, got the bottle out of the bag, cracked the seal, and set it in his lap. He looked to his left and right, and in the rearview. The smell of the booze was irresistible—like a serum that was going to cure all his ailments. Seeing no one, he put the bottle to his lips and took a swig. The forty-four-proof liquid burned going down and singed his nostrils. He quietly set the bottle back in his lap and sat there. He normally didn't drink it straight—nor in such stealth—and he felt a shadow of failure sweep over him.

His phone buzzed. He got it out and saw it was Janet calling.

"Hello," he answered.

"Hey, the counselor I want can't see us for like three weeks," she said. "She emailed me late last night. I just got it."

"That's not good. Aren't there any others we could try?"

"From what I'm finding, they're all booked out like that. I went ahead and made an appointment with her, but I wanted to check with you on the date and time."

She gave him the information and he checked the calendar on his phone and told her he would make it work.

"Are you at work?" she said. "You left early."

"I actually went to an AA meeting this morning."

Silence.

"I'm not quite to work yet," he said.

"How was it?" she said. "Where was it?"

He was about to tell her that compared with those heavy drinkers he didn't think he was an alcoholic, but then he reflected on where he was, and what he was doing, and he took pause.

"Presbyterian church on Wabash," he said. "It was . . . enlightening. Not sure I'd go back."

"I see," she said in a tone of disappointment.

"Have you heard anything from Nick?" he changed the subject.

"No. Have you?"

He was in the middle of taking another swig and hoped she hadn't heard the gin swish in the bottle.

"No," he said, wiping his mouth. "How are you feeling? Did you sleep well?"

"It's hard to sleep with the arm. It hurts."

"I bet. I'm sorry about that. Are you taking the acetaminophen?"

"More than I should."

"How's the head?"

"Better."

Tidwell realized he hadn't told Janet about Wayne Deetz getting shot the day before, so he filled her in. As they talked about it, Tidwell sealed the bottle, set it in the passenger seat, and began driving toward police headquarters.

The conversation was winding down.

Tidwell was feeling comfortably buzzed. He unwrapped the mints and popped three into his mouth and asked Janet what she had planned for the day, wondering if she had communicated any more with the mystery man.

"Rest," she said. "I might try to take the dog for a short walk, get some fresh air, if it doesn't rain all day."

"Any plans to talk to your old friend Greg today?"

Tidwell held his breath, knowing he shouldn't have said it.

After several moments, the phone clicked.

Janet had ended the call.

Tidwell cursed as loudly as he could and bashed the interior ceiling of the car. Then he did it again and again—until he was crying.

18

"GIRL TROUBLE?" Rickert said.

The last thing Brandon needed to contend with at that moment were inquiries from Rickert of all people; he barely knew the man.

"Eh, kind of," Brandon said as he drove the Interceptor down Cloverleaf. He could not get the photograph of Kristen and his dad out of his mind.

What on earth is she doing?

Kristen had seemed so perfect all these weeks. Well, not perfect. Her dysfunctional home life had concerned Brandon, but he'd never seen any sign of trouble with Kristen—until now. Her actions the night before and that morning had revealed a different side of her he'd never seen before, and it was bothering him so much it was tying knots in his stomach. He needed to talk to her, but it would have to wait until after work.

"Women are a pain in the rear," Rickert blurted. "Take it from someone who knows. Been married twice and both ended in disaster. One's still trying to rob me blind."

Brandon wondered if Deborah—the driver of the swerving car who'd gotten them ambushed the day before—would be let out on bail. If so, what would happen to her? Would they try again?

"You're not married yet, correct?" Rickert said.

"No, sir."

"Never do it. Save yourself a ton of heartache and money. You can love 'em, sure—but love 'em and leave 'em. It makes life so much easier. More fun, too."

This guy is such a windbag.

"I have one son who's just like his old lady. So full of himself. Can't take advice. Never listens. Off in Montana somewhere. Wants nothing to do with the old man. His mom says he has 'mental health issues.'" Rickert laughed. "The real problem is, he won't put on his big boy pants and work a steady job."

Brandon noticed two Black kids hurriedly spraying and wiping the windows of an SUV that was stopped at a traffic light. Kids in several parts of the city pulled this stunt—washing car windows without asking, then pretty much demanding the drivers pay for their services.

Rickert noticed it too and perked up.

"Stop those little punks!" he pointed at them. "Get up there and let me out!"

Rickert twisted in his seat like he was about to jump out of the car.

Brandon worked the Interceptor toward the intersection and, when they were about fifty feet away, Rickert made the siren chirp several times.

Both boys froze and looked up at the squad car at the same time. They looked to be fifteen or sixteen years old.

Rickert was out the door and heading toward them and Brandon followed quickly.

The taller of the two boys dropped his spray bottle and started to run toward two bicycles lying in the dirt, but Rickert drew his gun and pointed at him. "Stop!" he yelled. The boy kept running and Rickert fired a round into the air, which shocked Brandon. The boy dove to the ground and froze, screaming for Rickert not to shoot.

"Stay right there!" Rickert yelled. "Don't move!"

The tall boy lay there with his hands in the air.

The other boy had frozen where he was.

The car whose windshield they'd cleaned had sped away.

"Now get back over here with your buddy," Rickert ordered the tall kid.

"We weren't doing nothing wrong," said the smaller of the two, who wore a gray Chicago Bears hoodie and black Nike sweats.

The tall boy—who wore a light blue T-shirt and red shorts down to his calves with huge high-tops, got up and went back to the smaller kid and told him to keep his mouth shut.

Rickert holstered his gun but kept his right hand on it as he approached the boys. "Do we need to arrest you to make you stop doing this?" he said with his barrel chest puffed out. "Why don't you boys get jobs? McDonald's. Car wash. Anyplace."

"Pay's crap," the smaller boy said.

"Where do you live?" Brandon asked.

"Conklin," the smaller of the two said.

"There's plenty of businesses there. Get jobs!" Rickert said.

Brandon was next to Rickert now and planned to just let him handle it. To him, this was small potatoes.

"What *don't* you understand about *not* washing car windows when no one asked you to? Then demanding money? It's a crime. You're robbing people. And it ain't gonna continue while I'm out here."

The short kid mumbled something to the taller kid, who shook his head frantically to shut the kid up.

"What did you say?" Rickert stepped toward the smaller kid.

"I said, 'You're one to talk.' I recognize you."

Brandon's antennae went up.

Rickert's head ratcheted back and he squinted at the kid.

"He does not," the taller boy said nervously. "Just let us go, okay? We won't do it again. Please."

Rickert glanced at Brandon then looked back at the boys.

"Recognize me, from where?" Rickert said.

"You know where," the small boy said. "Theater."

Rickert's head swiveled—first to Brandon, then the tall kid, then back to the short one. For a flash, Rickert was speechless.

Brandon wondered what the heck was going on. Did the kid mean the theater where Lance Burke was gunned down?

"What theater?" Brandon blurted.

Rickert shot a glare at Brandon then back to the kid.

"He knows what I'm talking about," the smaller boy nodded

toward Rickert. "You gonna let us go, or you gonna take us in and let me tell them about what we seen that night?"

"What are you talking about?" Brandon inched closer to the boy. "Are you talking about when an officer got shot?" He glanced at Rickert who was frozen with a scowl on his stone face.

"Hey!" Rickert blared to drown out everyone else. "What would these little street urchins know about anything? Get out of here you punks. And if I ever see you doing this again, consider yourselves arrested."

The boys looked at each other and the tall one nodded the 'let's get out of here' sign to his friend. With their heads down they shuffled about, gathered their spray bottles and rolls of paper towels, and meandered off at a snail's pace toward their bikes.

Brandon had a feeling he would be wise to know where both boys lived and said to the taller one, "Do you live in Conklin too?"

"Who cares?" Rickert roared.

Brandon eyed Rickert, who cussed and mumbled something about "punks," and turned and headed for the cruiser.

Brandon felt his face flush.

The boy had said he recognized Rickert. He'd mentioned a theater and what he'd seen there. Why wasn't Rickert curious?

"What was that about, I wonder?" Brandon called to Rickert, determined to get more out of Rickert.

Rickert laughed without turning around. "Little brats would say anything. They're born learning how to lie around here."

Just then, as the boys were peddling away, the smaller of the two turned around toward the officers and waved his hand in the shape of a gun. He was yelling something unintelligible.

"Let's get out of here," Rickert said loudly.

The taller boy reached for the smaller one's arm, knocking it out of the air, and commanded him to keep riding.

The smaller boy yelled one last thing from which Brandon was able to decipher only one word before the boys were out of earshot —the word was "witnesses."

19

THE FIRST THING Tidwell did when he arrived at Portland Police Bureau headquarters was duck into the men's locker room and rinse his mouth out by hand with water. Feeling a good buzz, he stuffed three sticks of gum in his mouth, rather unsteadily changed into his uniform, and headed for his office.

On the way, almost everyone asked him how Janet was doing after her car wreck. As head of the unit, he felt obligated to stop and address each person, even if briefly, keeping his distance as he did so.

By the time he made it to his office—which had large glass walls overlooking dozens of cubicles—he felt as if he'd worked a whole day. He shut the door, fired up his computer, plunked down in his cushy swivel chair, hid behind the monitor, and gathered his thoughts.

He wondered if Janet's car wreck had made the news; he hadn't seen any reporters at the scene. He wondered if the kid who hit Janet had lived or not.

Tidwell replayed the morning phone conversation with Janet in his mind and shook his head in disgust, thinking he must have sounded like a jealous, pouting schoolboy when he had asked if she planned to talk to Stovall.

Maybe I should call and apologize . . .

Out the corner of his eye Tidwell spotted Detective Angie Cook and Assistant Head of Homicide Sid Sikorski making their way to his door.

Tidwell cursed under his breath. He forced a smile, leaned back in his squeaky chair, and waved them in before they even got to the door.

After small talk about Janet's condition, Sid and Angie said they wanted to talk about what had happened to Wayne and Brandon Deetz the day before in Edgewood. Tidwell had them sit down in the two chairs across from his desk.

"We've got an address on the deceased," Angie said.

"The kid Brandon shot?" Tidwell said.

"Right. He lives in a house on Traymont, not far from where the shooting happened. Brandon and Rickert are in the area." Angie glanced at Sid. "We think they should stop in there, see who else might live there, and what they can find."

Tidwell nodded. "Yeah, do it."

"We're also concerned about the girl who was driving the car," Sid said. "Deborah Fugate, twenty-four, from Olympia, Washington—"

"What do you mean, 'concerned?'" Tidwell said.

"We think she's going to need protection if she gets out on bail this morning," Sid said.

"Protection?" Tidwell laughed. "Since when are we in that business?"

"Sarge, that car she was driving was registered to Sidney Grimaldi," Angie said.

"So what?" Tidwell said. "That girl brought this on herself."

"Normally I'd feel the same, Sarge," Sid said, "but Sidney Grimaldi? He's one of the most notorious—"

"You don't have to tell me who he is, Sid. Come on, guys. What are the chances of her getting bailed out, anyway? Is there money in her family?"

Angie and Sid both shrugged. "We don't know," Angie said, "but it's obvious Grimaldi doesn't want her alive. We got a call from Brandon this morning and he's thinking the same thing."

"They are not going to plan a hit the second she walks down the courthouse steps," Tidwell said. "What do you propose we do, anyway, set up a security detail for her? Be her secret service? She's a criminal."

Tidwell realized he was sounding sloppy and made up his mind to reset.

"Look, seriously, what are you asking me? If she gets out on bail, what do you want to do?"

"It's not that big a deal, Sarge, we just want to follow her for a bit," Sid said.

Angie said, "Not only to make sure she's safe, but to see where she goes. See if she might lead us to the bigger fish."

This just all seemed so petty to Tidwell. And so unnecessary. The chick was a drug addict from Edgewood. The whole thing frustrated him. He stood up with a grunt.

"Guys, no. That is not on us. Yes, send Deetz and Rickert to the dead kid's house, for sure. That's a solid lead. But for us to follow this loser around Portland, no."

Tidwell walked around his desk to end the meeting. "Is that it?"

Angie and Sid looked at each other and stood up to leave.

"I appreciate you guys," Tidwell said. "Keep me posted."

Tidwell smelled nicotine on Angie, who was a known chain-smoker, and hoped he hadn't gotten too close to her; hoped she hadn't smelled the gin.

Sid and Angie were gracious as they left.

Discussions and disputes like this happened all the time.

No big deal.

Tidwell yawned and popped another mint into his mouth as he walked to the glass window overlooking all the cubicles. Off to the right—perhaps they thought out of his sight—Angie and Sid stood very close to one another in a serious discussion. Angie even covered her mouth with her notepad as she spoke so no one could read her lips.

Just as Tidwell was about to step away, Sid turned around and looked into Tidwell's office.

The two men's eyes locked.

Sid quickly turned away.

He leaned close to Angie and whispered something.

Without looking back at Tidwell, Angie and Sid set their shoulders back and took off in opposite directions.

20

FOR SOME REASON, Rickert insisted on driving after he and Brandon had run off the window-washer boys. It was as if driving was going to help him blow off steam and remind Brandon who was boss. Brandon didn't mind and it gave him a chance to text his mom to see how his dad was doing. In less than a minute she texted back:

> In pain. Grumpy. No appetite. But says he wants to get back to work! LOL.

Brandon couldn't stop thinking about the boys back there—how the tall one kept forcing the shorter one to be quiet. They knew something about the night Lance Burke died. They recognized Rickert. They had something on him. This felt big. And it made Brandon a bit nervous around Rickert.

Brandon looked over at the veteran cop, whose chiseled face was fixed on the road. Looking more closely at Rickert's ear, Brandon slowly leaned closer and squinted. There was a line on Rickert's earlobe the shape of a smile, which was a different color than the rest of his ear. That was the infamous scar he'd heard about.

"What're you lookin' at?" Rickert turned suddenly and glared at Brandon.

"Nothing."

Brandon needed to tell his Dad about what those boys had said.

Static filled the car and the voice of Sid Sikorski came over the radio. Brandon took the call and Sid informed him and Rickert that he had an address on the guy Brandon had shot the day before. Sid wanted them to check it out, see if anyone else lived there, and search the place if they could.

Just as Brandon ended the call and Rickert turned the Interceptor around and headed in the direction of the house of the deceased, Brandon's phone vibrated. It was a call. Rickert heard it and looked at Brandon, who glanced at the screen. It was Kristen.

He'd told her repeatedly not to call him while he was working unless it was an emergency.

Brandon heaved a sigh and sent the call to voicemail.

"She won't leave you alone, will she?" Rickert said with a chuckle.

Brandon feigned a laugh.

All of the sudden the relationship with Kristen had taken a whacky turn for the worse. A week ago, Brandon pictured himself possibly asking Kristen to marry him within the next year; now he was questioning her mental stability.

"You can take that," Rickert said, nodding toward Brandon's phone.

"Eh, not necessary," Brandon mumbled, thinking there was no way he was going to have a conversation with Kristen when he was sitting right next to Rickert.

Brandon's phone buzzed. He checked it. She'd left a voicemail, which made his heart rate spike. He flicked over and read the transcription: "Hi sweetie. Your dad is one tough hombre. And your mom is equally as tough. Now I see where you get it. I love your family. Tammy and J.P. were arriving when I left, so I got to visit with them for a few minutes. Your brother reminds me of your dad. Anyway, I'm off to work. How about dinner tonight? Love you."

He laughed to himself and looked out the passenger window.

Talk about Jekyll and Hyde.

"Okay, this is going to be it up here on the left, three or four more houses," Rickert said. "You ready?"

"Yes, sir." Brandon put his phone away.

The sky had turned a marble gray and it was starting to drizzle. The street had large potholes and most of the houses were trailers with dirt driveways and satellite dishes. They passed a long, wide ditch filled with standing water from the last rain, and a cluster of weathered mailboxes, each one leaning in a different direction.

Brandon couldn't imagine living there.

"Edgewood at its finest," Rickert said. "You ain't gonna find nothing good in this neighborhood. Nothing."

A girl and a boy, both about ten, raced by them on their bikes, standing up as they peddled, looking back every few seconds.

The Interceptor slowed.

"That's it, the light blue one." Rickert pointed to it.

The light blue trailer had an enormous, crooked antenna on the roof, was missing all but one shutter, and its driveway was riddled with puddles. A gold Saturn featuring one of those skinny spare tires was backed in right next to the trailer, close to the white metal awning that hung over the door.

"Car's backed in to hide the plates," Rickert said. "We'll block him in, just in case."

The Interceptor slowly rocked and bounced as Rickert eased it into the driveway and stopped about three feet from the bumper of the Saturn.

"How about you drop around back, just in case, and I'll go to the door," Rickert said. "What was the dead guy's name again?"

"Jesse Salvador."

Rickert mumbled a derogatory slang term, opened his door, and said, "Let's go."

Brandon got out.

"Hey," Rickert said, making eye contact with Brandon. "Use these." He held up his radio earpiece and plugged it into his left ear so they could communicate quietly without having their radios blaring. Brandon did the same.

With his eyes on the door, then the windows, Brandon made his way along the side of the weathered house.

"Radio check. You copy?" Rickert said quietly.

"Affirmative," Brandon said.

"Let me know when you're in position."

"Copy that," Brandon said.

Brandon made his way along the side of the dilapidated house. When he was about to round the rear corner he heard Rickert cuss and turned around to see him trying to wipe a glob of wet mud off his black boots.

Brandon turned the corner, walked, and in about ten feet came to a dirty window. He peeked inside and pressed the button of the microphone on the wire at his neck and whispered, "Two men are sitting at a small table in the kitchen, both white. I can't make out details, the window's dirty."

Brandon drew his Glock.

"Copy," Rickert said.

A dog barked from inside and Brandon saw it get up and scamper across the kitchen; it was dark, medium-sized.

The men began to look around as if the dog had heard something and one of them stood.

"I'm in position," Brandon whispered.

"Copy you," Rickert said. "I'm at the door."

Brandon then heard Rickert pound on the door and announce himself as police.

The other man inside shot to his feet.

Brandon's heart raced as he mentally prepared for one or both of them to fly out the back door, which was only twelve feet from him.

One of the men took several steps toward the front door, peered out, and dashed back to the other man. He'd seen Rickert at the door. The man barked an order to the other tall man who disappeared with giant strides into a back hallway.

The man in view fixed his hair, looked down, straightened his shirt, and headed for the door.

"One of them went into a back hallway," Brandon said into his mic. "The other one is coming to the door."

"Copy," Rickert said. "Just stay back there and make sure he doesn't leave."

"Copy." Brandon stood by the window with his eyes locked on the hallway where the tall guy went. He could hear Rickert speaking to the one who answered the door.

After about a minute, Rickert addressed Brandon over the radio:

"Come in through the back door and find the other guy. I got this one."

Brandon hurried to the rickety screen door, turned the knob, and found the door locked.

"It's locked. You want me to force entry or come around front?"

"Come to the front," Rickert said. "Make it fast."

Brandon sprinted along the side of the house to the door under the metal awning where Rickert had entered. He plunged into the house. Rickert had his weapon drawn on the man who had answered the door, who stood coolly with his hands in the air. He was about twenty-five with brown hair, average build, and clean-cut.

With his gun locked out in front of him, Brandon went by them toward the back hallway. "Police!" he yelled. "Come out with your hands where I can see them!" He slowed and waited at the opening of the small hallway. Hearing nothing, he started down the hall with his weapon in front of him. A toilet ran in a tiny bathroom to the left as if it had just been flushed. Only one doorway remained at the end of the short hall.

"Police!" Brandon yelled. "Come out, hands high!"

This is all I need, to kill a third person.

He dashed over and positioned himself just outside the room with his back to the wall and gun up by his chest. He stuck his arm out into the doorway to see if it would draw gunfire, but it didn't. He took a deep breath, exhaled through an o-shaped mouth, and turned the corner into the room, leading the way with the Glock.

No one.

Small room. Red walls. Cheap twin beds. Nightstand. Gray shag carpet. Window . . . *open!*

Brandon dashed for the window and looked out.

A tall man was running from the house, toward the woods. At that split-second, the man turned around toward the house.

He saw Brandon and Brandon saw him.

For Brandon, it was as if he'd heard the shutter of a camera clicking.

Brandon recognized the man.

Then everything went back into motion.

"Runner!" he yelled as he took off for the back door, figuring it would be faster than getting through the window.

Brandon unlocked the back door, threw open the screen door, jumped down the back steps, and took off for the woods.

"Stop, police!" he yelled as he ran, knowing he wasn't going to be able to catch up to Nick Tidwell.

21

TIDWELL HUNG up his office phone after speaking with a reporter about a civil case currently in the news. Normally, he detested such calls, but he welcomed this one simply because he didn't want to be bothered by anyone and the call made him appear busy. He had his office door closed, he had a splitting headache, and his mind was a million miles away from police work.

With pen in hand and paperwork in front of him, he doodled as he kept thinking about the AA meeting earlier that morning and the freakish odds of running into the guy he'd run off the road—Neil Houser. That was the type of unthinkable 'coincidence' that made Tidwell wonder if God could indeed be at work behind everything.

And Janet! What had happened to them? They'd had the storybook marriage. They'd been life partners. Tidwell couldn't fathom that she was interested in another man. Somewhere in the recesses of his mind, way back in the cobwebs, something told him that their troubles were his fault. Working way too many hours. Caring more about police work than about his wife. Drinking way too often and, perhaps, too much at times.

Tidwell tossed the pen down and looked at his watch. It was late morning. He needed to see Deetz. After all, the old guy had been shot, which was the ideal excuse to skip out of the office in the middle of the day. Tidwell needed to finish updating Deetz about what was going on with Janet. Deetz always had good advice.

As the big man gathered his things, his mouth watered when he thought of the bottle of gin in the car, giving him even more incentive to clear out of there for a long lunch.

Tidwell flipped off the light, left his office, and closed the door. With his jacket over his arm, he headed down the hall toward his car when he heard Sid Sikorski's voice from the opposite direction.

"Hey Sarge. Where you headed?"

Frustrated that he'd not made it out cleanly, Tidwell stopped, turned around, and faced Sid with a silent groan. "Going to see Deetz." The courteous thing would have been to invite Sid to tag along, but Tidwell wanted to be alone.

"You got a quick second?" Sid nodded toward Tidwell's office.

Tidwell stared at him momentarily and thought about saying he really had to go, but Sid likely meant it when he said it would be brief. Plus, Sid had a rare, deathly serious look on his face.

Without a word, Tidwell sauntered back into his office, hit the light, turned around, and sat on the edge of his desk with his jacket folded over his crossed arms. Sid followed him in, turned his back to Tidwell, and quietly closed the door.

That never happened.

"Wow, this must be important," Tidwell said, feeling slightly uneasy about what might be coming.

Sid inhaled deeply as he walked over to Tidwell and exhaled with an audible sigh when he was standing within three feet of the boss.

"I smelled booze on you earlier," Sid said.

Tidwell looked at Sid for a moment, then dropped his head to his chest. His face flushed and he instantly thought he was going to lose his job—on top of everything else.

"Angie did, too," Sid said.

No.

When Tidwell said nothing, Sid crossed to one of the two guest chairs and sat down on the front edge. "We agreed to keep it to ourselves, but Sarge, if you're drinking in the morning, you need to get help." Sid looked up at the tall man, sympathetically.

Tidwell slowly lifted his chin, set his coat aside, rubbed his eyes and face, and rested his large hands on the desk to either side of him.

"I don't know what to say to you, Sid. I'm sorry. And I'm embarrassed. Janet and I have hit a really rough patch. Of course, that's no excuse."

"I don't know if I ever told you," Sid said, "but one of my brothers has been in AA for over six years. It's been a lifeline for him. Maybe that could help you."

"Huh." Tidwell crossed his arms. "You're not going to believe this, but I went to my first AA meeting this morning, the very morning I then go and decide to drink on the job. I want you to know, this is the first time."

Sid shook his head. "You don't owe me any explanations, Sarge. But I'm concerned about others finding out. You're too good of a leader; we can't afford to lose you."

Tidwell nodded, then cussed and shook his head in disgust. "I've let you guys down. I apologize, Sid. It's nothing but weakness. I'm letting my personal life spill over into my work. It's inexcusable."

Sid stood. "Sarge, you're the best thing that's ever happened to the bureau. We need you. If there's anything I can do, I'm here for you."

Tidwell reached out and rested a hand atop Sid's left shoulder. "Thank you, man. It's not going to happen again. I should talk to Angie."

"You can if you want, but she's cool. We're on your side, Sarge."

Tidwell nodded and guided Sid to the door.

As Sid left, Tidwell said, "I appreciate you."

Next, he texted Angie, who showed up to his office within two minutes. Tidwell apologized to her and made the same promise he'd made to Sid, that it wouldn't happen again.

As Tidwell headed for his car he realized the problems with the promise he'd made to Angie and Sid: number one, he wasn't positive he could keep the promise not to drink again on the job, and number two, he wasn't sure he wanted to, either.

22

THE ONE AND only reason Tidwell fought off the temptation to hit the gin on the way to Wayne Deetz's house was Deetz himself. In Tidwell's mind, Deetz was everything good—devout father, husband, and friend. He was honest and trustworthy to the core. He did what was right. And he was freakishly generous with his time and money. Tidwell couldn't bring himself to take the chance of having Deetz smell liquor on him in the middle of the day.

Leena answered the door and Tidwell gave her a bear hug and they did their usual bantering back and forth.

The house was cozy, as usual, and a pleasant aroma of something cooking drifted in from the kitchen.

"So, I guess you're here to see the wounded warrior," Leena said. "That's what Mom's calling him."

Tidwell chuckled. Leena had the best sense of humor. "Indeed I am. I bet you're taking excellent care of him."

"You know I am. I'm a whole lot more patient than Mom is, that's for sure. Dad said I have an exceptional bedside manner."

"I'm sure you do. Maybe you should think about becoming a nurse."

"Meh." Leena made a sour face. "I wouldn't want to do this for just anyone. It gets old."

Tidwell held back his laughter. "No?"

"Nah," Leena said. "It's tough enough taking care of your own family members. I'm sticking with the chicken business. Did I tell you they made me one of the leads in the drive-thru?"

"No. Get out of town."

Leena nodded proudly. "We set a record last month for most cars through the drive-thru during lunch hours. The owner gave everyone on the drive-thru team a twenty-five-dollar gift card to the new frozen yogurt shop at Pioneer Place."

"Man!" Tidwell said. "You are a rock star."

"Yep. My goal is to become the head of the whole drive-thru. Dad says I can do it if I keep my shoulder to the grindstone . . . kind of an old person's cliché. You've heard it, right?"

"Oh sure, sure. I'm old school. I get it."

"Well look who's here." Joanie came into the living room wiping her hands on a dish towel. "You're just in time for Wayne's favorite soup. Can I get you a bowl, Dolby?"

"Mmm. Smells incredible," Tidwell said.

"Speaking of chicken, it's enchilada chicken soup," Leena said. "Truly not bad."

Joanie nodded with eyebrows raised.

"I might have some—after I see the patient," Tidwell said.

"J.P. and Tammy are in there now, but they're just leaving. How's Janet?" Joanie said.

Tidwell explained how Janet was progressing, physically, but felt like he was hiding a million secrets behind his cool façade.

Leena crossed to the master bedroom, clapped her hands, and leaned in the doorway. "Okay kids, that's a wrap. Time to move along. The old guy has another visitor. They just keep coming."

Leena looked at Tidwell and said, "We had an unexpected visitor earlier. It was this girl Brandon's been seeing, and wow—"

"That's enough, Leena," Joanie said. "No need to get into that."

Leena lifted a hand to cover her mouth from her mom and said to Tidwell, "Let's just say it was . . . bizarre at best."

J.P. and Tammy came out of Deetz's room and made pleasantries with Tidwell, while Joanie and Leena went in to check on Deetz.

"Hey, did Wayne pass that info on to you for Nick?" Tammy asked Tidwell. "About The Morning 7s and Redeeming Recovery?"

"He did. Thanks for sending that," Tidwell said. "I passed it along. Now it's up to Nick."

J.P. asked how Janet was recovering and Tidwell updated Tammy and him on her progress.

"Okay!" Leena came out of Deetz's room with a joyful bounce in her step. "The old guy says if it was anyone else it would be a hard no, but since it's the great Sergeant Tidwell, he will see you now."

Joanie came out next and said, "He's all yours, Dolby. I'm going to bring him soup while you guys talk. You want some?"

Tidwell looked at his watch and figured this would be lunch.

"Sure. Thanks, Joanie."

"Don't be too hard on him, he's tired," Joanie said.

"I will not stay long, I promise."

Deetz was sitting up in bed leaning back against several pillows. He wore a crisp, light blue pajama top. The blinds were open and the light reflected off his glasses. The graying hair on his temples was messy and his face looked a bit gaunt, but for being gunned down a day ago, Deetz looked surprisingly chipper.

"What is this? You stay home from work just because you get shot?" Tidwell jested as he approached the bed and gave Deetz a palm-to-palm handshake.

"Believe me, I'd rather be working," Deetz said. "Sit."

"I'm not staying long." Tidwell pulled up a chair and sat. "I think Joanie will make sure of that. And Leena. That kid is a hoot."

Deetz smiled with a sigh, reached for a silver thermal mug, and sipped from the straw.

"How are you?" Tidwell said.

"Rough night," Deetz said. "Every inch of me was sore. Today's better. The pain is all in the leg now."

"What are they gonna do, give you one of those scooters you push around with your leg in the seat?"

"No. I bashed my knee and it's not going to bend for a while." He nodded toward a pair of crutches leaning in the corner. "They gave me those."

"Mmm. That's a pain. What do they say about your recovery time?"

"Doctor said we'll talk about that tomorrow. I go back for a follow-up. I'll have rehab come in for sure. You know me, I can't sit around very long."

"Yoo-hoo." Leena entered, followed by Joanie. Each carried a tray with a bowl of steaming soup, tortilla chips, spoons, and napkins. "One tray for each copper," Leena said.

Tidwell stood to be polite but they had him sit right back down, getting each man set up with a tray and soup.

"Wow, does that look good, ladies," Tidwell said. "Thanks so much."

"Thanks, girls," said Deetz.

"Bon appétit," Leena said as she whirled around, staggered, and left the room.

Joanie laughed and followed her.

"We found a residence for the guy Brandon shot," Tidwell said. "We've got Brandon and Rickert heading out there now to check it out."

"Let me bless it for us really quick," Deetz said.

"Oh, yeah, sure, sure," Tidwell said, kicking himself for not remembering that Deetz always did that.

"Lord Jesus, thanks for this food, our health, our loved ones, and all our provisions. Be with Dolby and Janet and Nick; shine your favor on them. Be alive and real to Dolby and give him your peace and direction. Help me heal quickly. And bless the blue today. Amen."

"Amen," Tidwell mumbled.

"So, what about the girl who was driving?" Deetz said. "Did she get bail?"

Tidwell shrugged. "Don't know yet. Everyone's making a big deal of it."

"Brandon said that car they were in is registered to Sidney Grimaldi."

"Right. He probably has a hundred cars in his name." Tidwell blew on a spoonful of soup and slurped it in. "Mmm. Wow, is that good."

"Sarge, Grimaldi put a hit out on that girl," Deetz said. "She knows something; something big."

"Wayne, we're not in the security business."

"Don't you think we should at least put a tail on her?" Deetz said, stirring his soup to cool it.

"Why am I the only one who *doesn't* want to do that?"

"Good question. Maybe you ought to rethink it."

"We'll see," Tidwell said, thinking if Deetz was in favor, maybe he should reconsider. Deetz always had the Midas touch.

They ate their soup while making small talk.

"How's Nick?" Deetz said.

Tidwell shrugged. "Haven't heard from him. I did pass along those recovery places Tammy sent. Thanks for that."

"Sure. So, how are things between you and Janet?"

Tidwell shook his head. "Not good. A mess, actually. I need to get my act together."

"That night at the hospital you were in the middle of telling me about finding Janet's phone in her car . . . and where she might've been going."

Tidwell squinted with a pained expression, ran a large hand over his bald head, and stretched as he debated how much to tell Deetz. "She was on her way to meet an old classmate for dinner. A guy. Rich guy."

"Classmate from—"

"High school."

"Man. I'm sorry."

"Yeah. He's divorced—from an attorney. Big-time architect; designs skyscrapers all over the place. Looks like Robert Redford. Name's Greg Stovall."

"How long's this been going on?"

"She said six weeks, but who knows?" Tidwell leveled his gaze at Deetz. "They've done video calls."

Deetz groaned and shook his head.

"You guys need to get counseling."

"The one she wants us to see is booked three weeks out."

"That's okay, you need to do it. Go ahead and book it."

Tidwell nodded. "According to her, I'm an alcoholic and a workaholic."

Deetz looked silently into Tidwell's eyes.

"She may be right," Tidwell said.

Silence fell over the room as the two men finished their soup.

"I'm not sure you know this or remember, but I used to really struggle with anxiety," Deetz said. "It paralyzed me at times."

Tidwell said nothing but had a hunch Deetz was going to steer the conversation toward religion again. And Deetz was about the only person in the world who Tidwell would listen to on that subject—but not for long.

"When J.P. and Tammy invited us to church and I started listening to the messages and reading the Bible, I realized God didn't want me to fret or to be anxious or to worry anymore. I learned I was his child. You're his child, too, man. He cares about you."

Deetz said these things with such emotion that his eyes glistened and it mesmerized Tidwell.

"I started writing down Bible verses and memorizing them to help me combat the anxiety," Deetz said.

Tidwell just stared at him.

"My favorite one says, 'God hasn't given me a spirit of fear—but of love, and power, and a sound mind.' That really helped me. Every time I began to get anxious, I'd say to myself, 'Wait, he hasn't given me a spirit of fear. He's given me a spirit of love, power, sound mind. As I started to believe his love for me and to have faith that he's real and wants the best for me, I began to overcome the anxiety."

"You know, Wayne." Tidwell sighed loudly, set his tray aside, and leaned forward with his forearms resting on his knees. "I believe that. I see that in you. You are the most Christian person I know. I respect you more than anyone."

"God can help you, Dolby. He cares about you the same way."

But Tidwell was not like Deetz. Tidwell was an unstable, angry man, and he was ashamed of himself. He thought of the bottle of gin in his car, the failed AA meeting and Neil Houser, and of Sid's confrontation with him that morning. He thought of the marriage he was about to lose and of the unstable son he'd raised. His only real success had been his work—and now that was in jeopardy.

"Why don't you go to my church tomorrow," Deetz said. "I won't be there, obviously, but just go by yourself. Nine or eleven. You know where it is. Maybe Janet would want to go."

Tidwell dropped back in his chair with a huff.

Going to church was not what he had in mind for his day off.

He wondered if Janet would even consider going with him. He honestly didn't know what her response would be if he asked her. And she may not be up for it anyway, in her condition.

He could go alone. Sit way in the back. Be anonymous.

"It's online too, if you don't want to go in person," Deetz said.

Tidwell's phone vibrated in his pocket. It was a call.

Good, he thought. *That gets me off the hook.*

He dug it out of his pocket and examined the screen.

"Let me take this, Wayne. It's Sid."

Tidwell stood, turned his back to Deetz, and answered the call.

"Deborah Fugate is dead, Sarge," Sid said. "She got out on bail, took an Uber to an extended stay motel, checked in, and got shot five minutes later on her way to her second-story room."

Tidwell was instantly dizzy.

He bumped his chair away from Deetz and plunked down, starting to sweat.

"Virgil and Ben are out there now going over the crime scene and searching for any camera footage," Sid said.

Tidwell felt as if he might throw up.

That girl's blood was on his hands.

They'd all told him the girl should be tailed. But, while under the influence, he'd laughed it off. Mister big bad know-it-all had laughed it off.

Now the girl was on her way to the morgue.

And Tidwell was stone cold sober with guilt.

"Sarge?" Sid said.

"How old was she," Tidwell said in monotone.

"Let's see, born in ninety-nine, so she was twenty-four. I gotta go."

Silence.

Frazzled, Tidwell said, "I'm sorry, Sid. I should have listened—"

"I'll keep you updated, okay? Gotta run—"

"No, wait, I should have listened to you, to Angie—"

The line went dead.

Tidwell continued holding the phone to his ear in bewilderment.

He felt Deetz's eyes burning into him from behind like the eyes of God himself.

Deetz had probably figured out what had happened and Tidwell couldn't face him. Instead, Tidwell blurted that he had to go and asked Deetz to tell Joanie thanks. He stalked out of the room, embarrassed to be alive.

23

BRANDON GAVE CHASE, but as he'd thought, Nick Tidwell had too much of a jump on him and disappeared into the thick woods behind the ramshackle trailer where Rickert was still holding the other man inside.

On Brandon's way back, it began to rain harder and his mind reeled. Should he tell Rickert it was Sergeant Tidwell's son who had escaped? Brandon's dad was good friends with Tidwell, their families were close. If Brandon had more time, he would call his dad first and let him know what had happened; he would know what to do—perhaps let Sergeant Tidwell address the matter with Nick under the radar.

The problem was, Brandon didn't trust Rickert—not only because of the things Clarence and Deetz had said about him, but because of the run-in with those boys earlier. Those kids knew something about the night Lance Burke died and Brandon wondered what possibly could have happened; he needed to talk to his dad about that, too.

As Brandon approached the back door of the mobile home the dog began barking like crazy. Brandon entered and went directly to the small bathroom in the hallway. The small dog waddled in, wagging its tail. Brandon removed the lid of the toilet and looked behind the tank for drugs but found nothing.

"I take it you didn't catch him," Rickert said with a hint of disdain as Brandon entered the living area, the dog following closely behind him.

"No," Brandon said.

The man in custody sat in a worn, oversized gold corduroy chair with his head in his hands. He was white, clean-cut, with short brown hair.

"This one says he's an EMT," Rickert said with his thumbs in the front of his gun belt and his chest puffed out. "He owns the car out front. The other guy is his partner—work partner that is."

Brandon's dad had recently told him that Nick was an EMT, so that virtually confirmed that the man who got away was indeed Nick Tidwell.

"What are you guys doing here?" Brandon said to the man seated. "Whose place is this?"

The man raised his head and sat back in the chair with a sigh. He was thin with large blue eyes and a long, narrow face. "It's a friend's place," he said. "We were meeting for coffee, that's all. I have no idea what this is about."

Brandon ducked into the small kitchen to see if there was a coffee pot; there was, but it wasn't turned on. He returned to the living area. "What's the name of your friend who owns this place?"

After a long pause, the man said, "Skip."

"Skip who?" Rickert demanded.

"Manford."

Brandon wrote it down and said, "Do you know Jesse Salvador?"

"Never heard of him."

"Do you know Sidney Grimaldi?"

"No! I told your partner all this already."

"What you didn't tell us yet is your buddy's name—the one who ran. What's his name?" Rickert said.

Here it comes . . .

"Look, please, don't make me tell you that," the guy whined. "We haven't done anything wrong. Why am I even being detained?" He looked at his watch and stood. "I need to be someplace."

That got Rickert. He took three forceful strides toward the guy and got right in his face. "We'll tell you when you can leave, Marty."

Rickert turned to Brandon and laughed. "His name's Marty

Martin. Can you imagine?" Rickert turned back to the man. "What was your momma thinking, boy."

Brandon didn't like that kind of talk and went to look around some more. "Have you searched it all?" he said to Rickert.

"Affirmative," Rickert called.

As Brandon combed through a small, messy bedroom he overheard Rickert questioning the man further about the name of his EMT partner who had escaped.

The bedroom smelled of cigarettes and Brandon was grossed out as he lifted pillows, opened drawers, and kicked his way through piles of dirty clothes.

Brandon heard a struggle from the living room, then a distinct slap, a yelp from Marty, followed by Rickert demanding more information.

Brandon rushed back in to find Marty Martin half bent over, rubbing his jaw, and squinting at Rickert with hatred in his eyes.

"You'll never guess who ran out the back door," Rickert said to Brandon. "Not in a million years."

Marty Martin straightened up. His cheek was bright red. He stuck his hands to his waist, huffed, bent over, and shook his head.

"Who?" Brandon said.

"Our very own Sergeant Tidwell's son, Nick. Kid's always been trouble."

"Look, I really need to go," Marty said. "Can I please leave? You have all my information. Please."

Rickert jerked Marty by his collar, shook him, and spoke to the frightened man through clenched teeth. "You are so lucky we didn't find anything, Marty Martin." Rickert shoved Marty as hard as he could toward the door and Marty tripped and hit the ground hard. Rickert didn't let up. "Your day is coming Marty." Rickert kicked him in the rear and Marty sprawled out on the floor again. "You better clean up your act."

Rickert went for him again.

It was too much.

"That's enough!" Brandon yelled.

Both men's heads swiveled toward Brandon.

"Just go, man. Beat it," Brandon said to Marty.

Marty sprang to his feet like a puppet that had suddenly been yanked upright and bashed out the door in a blur.

Silence fell over the tight trailer and Brandon felt the flutter of butterflies low in his stomach, fully expecting Rickert's rebuttal.

"Why're you sticking up for that measly piece of trash?" Rickert's nostrils flared and he walked toward Brandon brashly, his dark eyes wide.

"That's *not* how I learned to do the job," Brandon said.

"Oh, it isn't, huh? I'll tell you what, boy, you do this job for thirty years *then* you tell me what you 'learned' in your little police academy."

Now Brandon bowed up.

It was the Rickerts of the country who gave police a bad name.

"Good police don't treat people like you treated him," Brandon said, almost out of breath he was so worked up. "It wasn't necessary." His heart thundered.

Rickert's top teeth bit his bottom lip and he winced as if in pain, apparently debating what to do next.

Brandon didn't care. This was the first time he'd worked with Rickert and he was determined to set a precedent that he was not going to put up with brutality or dirty policing.

"You're just like your old man." Rickert approached Brandon and jammed a finger in his face. "Officer goody two-shoes. The fruity Mister Rogers of the neighborhood."

Brandon's blood pounded in his veins like a raging river, but he said to himself repeatedly, *be calm, be smart.*

But when Rickert's finger actually pressed Brandon's nose, the kid exploded inside, knowing he had to do something. He quickly planned his detonation with precision.

He waited.

Rickert made another derogatory comment about Brandon's dad and touched his nose again, pleading for a fight.

Brandon raised both hands and moved one step backward as if retreating.

Time to make a stand.

The very millisecond Rickert's body language relented, Brandon took one commanding step toward the man and punched him in the gut with such lightning speed and force that they both heard the wind suck out of him as he bent over.

Brandon stepped back with his fists in the air, ready to fight, bouncing on his toes.

"I'm not putting up with that crap on my watch," he said. "There's a right way and a wrong way to do this job. I'll report you if I see any more of it."

Brandon was trembling and short of breath, but the adrenaline and Rickert's injury had him feeling invincible. Like a boxer raring to attack, he took several forceful steps toward Rickert, then backward, then forward, as if he wanted to pound the man into the ground. It was a mental trick Clarence had taught him to proactively freak out the opponent.

Rickert slowly straightened.

His pupils appeared ablaze.

His face was contorted in rage.

Brandon swallowed hard and lost some of his resolve.

Rickert stepped toward Brandon, who tensed and mentally prepared for a fight.

Rickert put up two fists that looked like wood block meat tenderizers. Brandon psyched himself up and worked his feet, backing up and stepping forward—but his confidence waned.

Rickert stood still, knees bent, fists up, like a boxer of old.

Brandon took a jab at Rickert's head, but Rickert's dodged it with surprising agility.

Uh oh.

Rickert then lifted and opened his left hand in front of his own face and—in one seamless blur of motion—spun around and cracked Brandon's jaw with a flying right elbow that clocked him like a steel rod.

Brandon dropped to the floor.

Dizzy.

Stunned.

He heard Rickert walk away.

The fight was over.

Seeing stars, Brandon felt his jaw, thinking it had to have been broken.

"You're fine," Rickert called. "Come on."

Brandon got to his knees.

The dog came over and licked him repeatedly.

His lip was bleeding.

Attempting to stand, he stumbled and steadied himself against the gold chair. He took some deep breaths.

Rickert had exited the mobile home and had left the door swaying in the rainswept breeze.

Brandon headed in that direction but was unsteady on his feet. His head felt wobbly, as if it was barely attached. He made it to the door, leaning on the doorframe to steady himself.

Rickert revved the engine in the rain. He stuck his head out the driver's window. "Let's go!"

24

TIDWELL WAS NUMB. He didn't know where he was going, he was just driving. The only sound was that of the intermittent sweeping of the windshield wipers and the occasional swishing of the gin in the bottle in the seat next to him.

He was cruising in the Charger along Davenport Drive, speed limit thirty-five—a long stretch of small, expensive houses with fancy non-serif address numbers on oversized brick mailboxes and sleek blacktop driveways, many of them circular. As he slowly cruised past the occasional small plaza with select high-end shops and eateries, his mind was somewhere else, somewhere it had never been his entire life.

That girl, Deborah Fugate, was dead, and it had been his decision not to put a tail on her—which could have saved her life.

That . . . and everything else.

He drove and he thought.

Could the alcohol be the root cause of the crucible he was in?

Would things improve if he quit drinking?

It was Saturday, July twenty-third. He could take a week or two off. He had plenty of sick days and vacation time. Forget the stupid job. He could find a detox facility and get sober. But, then again, he really believed he could quit on his own if he wanted to. It wasn't that much of a dependency. Besides, he enjoyed it, looked forward to it.

He came upon a small, old-fashioned looking church with only two cars in the parking lot, and he swung the Charger in and parked far away from the building and cars.

He turned the engine off and started searching local detox centers on his phone. There were many listings. Some were outpatient, some were inpatient. Some took insurance, some didn't. Some were science-based, some were religion-based. Some were centered on medications and some touted no medications. There was group therapy and private clinical care. There was twelve-step and non-twelve step. Some offered licensed clinicians with one-on-one therapy. A few even promised rapid recovery in as few as seven days.

Tidwell took in a deep breath, held it, set his shoulders back against the driver's seat, and exhaled slowly through his mouth. A woman in a navy rain jacket came out a door to what looked like the church office, put her hood up, and hurried to her car.

Tidwell reflected on what Deetz had said, the part about God giving him a sound mind. Peace. Tidwell did not have that now. The opposite was true. He was unsure of himself. He craved a drink to get him through. He felt sick with guilt and shame—about so many things.

One car besides his remained in the parking lot, over by the office. At the opposite end of the building, some hundred feet from the office, several steps led up to a large, dark wooden door—probably the sanctuary. In the old days, many churches remained open around the clock; anyone could go in and have a quiet moment. Nowadays, however, Tidwell guessed many were locked.

What the heck.

He got out of the car, locked it, and walked fast through the rain to the church building—not quite sure why he was doing so. He bounded up the steps and—moment of truth—the heavy door opened with a loud squeak.

Tidwell stepped inside and let his eyes adjust to the dark vestibule as the door clanked shut behind him. It smelled musky. Seven or eight candles burned brightly in small red glass jars, surrounded by many more unlit candles. He walked into the quiet sanctuary and stopped. The light from outside backlit the beautiful stained-glass windows that ran along both sides of the sanctuary.

Tidwell walked slowly up the center aisle on thick, old red carpet. The floor felt uneven. The pews were made of dark wood and were covered with long red velvet cushions. He glanced up at the pulpit and beyond to the altar and slender cross on the wall and took a seat at the end of one of the pews.

He bent over and rested his elbows on his knees and clasped his hands beneath his chin.

Silence.

Nothing but silence.

The walls of the old building seemed so thick, and the windows so brilliant, that he felt peacefully insulated from the chaotic world outside.

He closed his eyes.

"I've never given you the time of day," he whispered.

Long pause.

"I'm sorry about that." He remembered what Deetz had said about God wanting to help him. But Tidwell was not anything like Deetz; Deetz was good. "Look, I'm in trouble here. My wife, she means everything to me. I can't lose her."

A surge of emotion swelled up inside him and pricked his eyes.

"My son is not good . . . I feel like I've failed them both."

As he thought of his early morning purchase at the liquor store, and of Deborah Fugate's death, his head dropped to his chest.

He began to cry.

Tears of hopelessness. Of depression.

Tears of remorse and unworthiness and helplessness.

It felt so good to release everything, to cry, which Tidwell rarely did.

He hoped no one would come in.

He could sit there forever.

It was like his own private recovery chamber.

He felt as if all of his problems were draining out of him, away from him.

Of course, the door opened at that exact moment.

He didn't look back but wiped his tears on his sleeve, sniffed, and remained seated as the door shut hard behind him.

There were footsteps. Someone coming down the aisle. Then,

one of the wooden kneelers squeaked as someone unfolded it behind Tidwell, to his left.

Tidwell sighed, thinking he could have stayed nestled away in that catacomb all day. But whoever it was that came in had stirred him back to reality.

Tidwell stood thinking he had better get back to police bureau headquarters. He headed down the aisle and noticed the figure of a person kneeling to his right. He kept going toward the door and told himself he needed to come here again. Next time he would light a candle, even though he didn't know what that meant.

"Excuse me."

A soft male voice came from behind. It had to be the man kneeling. *Maybe he sneezed.*

Tidwell turned to face the man just before opening the door to leave.

The man had risen in the pew, was facing Tidwell, raising his hand as if wanting his attention.

"Were you talking to me?" Tidwell said.

"Yes," the man left his pew and, using an old wooden cane, began hobbling toward Tidwell. "Yes, I was." He had curly gray hair, white beard stubble, and cheeks that were crimson from the sun. His black suit was well wrinkled and he had on a crooked, black bowtie.

Tidwell rolled his eyes, wondering what the old coot wanted— probably a handout.

"My name is Tristan, Tristan Farnsworth. And you may be?" He spoke with an English accent and stopped within five feet of Tidwell, then leaned against the end of a pew, out of breath.

"Dolby. What can I do for you?" He glanced at his watch. "I'm in a bit of a hurry."

"Ah," Tristan raised his chin and cane at the same time, "the whole world is in a hurry, Dolby."

Tidwell noticed the man's brilliant eyes for the first time, which were the blue of a bluebird, and the whites as white as cotton.

"Well?" Tidwell said, "can I help you in some way?"

"There is something you need to know, Dolby. Can you stop for one moment? Can you be still?"

Oh, brother. For real?

"What is it, man? What do you want?" Tidwell said, obviously in a hurry.

"I want for nothing, Dolby. My soul is completely content. It is you who is lacking. Is it not? You're in trouble, aren't you?"

Tidwell turned away from the exit and squared up to the small man, narrowing his eyes at him, thinking he would be saying this to anyone dumb enough to listen.

"What makes you think I'm in trouble?"

The man looked down and rubbed his chin. He tapped his cane on the pew several times, tossed it up, snatched it, and leveled his gaze at Tidwell. "From the moment I opened my eyes this morning, I've had an overwhelming feeling of uneasiness. Something in my spirit has been nagging at me like a bugger."

Tidwell wondered how many people the old man tried this on.

"I had a doctor's appointment, then went to the library, all the while, watching and waiting like a sentry for God's direction."

As Tidwell listened, the man's large clear eyes and accent mesmerized him.

"Do you know, Dolby," Tristan pointed his cane toward the door, "I never come down this road—never. But something inside me today said, 'Turn on Davenport.'"

Tidwell felt uneasy.

Could this be legit?

"Then, 'Go into that church,'" Tristan continued. "Of course, I obeyed. I had no choice. I was completely burdened. The weight of the world was on me shoulders."

Tidwell could only stare at the man, waiting for more, thirsting for more.

"I assume you're in the Charger," Tristan said. "I saw the bottle on the passenger seat and knew I was in the right place."

This was either the con of a lifetime, or something supernatural was taking place.

"I have a word for you, Dolby. Now, you can choose to believe I'm just a senile old man, or you can take this for what it really is— a message from the Most High—something specific God wants you to hear, to know."

Tidwell shifted uncomfortably.

"Dolby, I'm not here for my health. I'm a servant. I'm obeying God. Today my job is to be his messenger."

"Yeah, but you could be doing this to anybody."

"Yes, but I'm not. He brought me here. To you. Today. Specifically."

"Okay, hit me. Then, I've really got to go."

Tristan stood up straight, set his shoulders back, and looked Tidwell in the eyes with such ferocity that the big man took a step back.

"I will lead the blind by ways they have not known. Along unfamiliar paths I will guide them. I will turn the darkness into light before them. And make the rough places smooth." Tristan paused and blinked and cleared his throat. "These are the things I will do; I will not forsake them."

Tristan tossed his cane again, snatched it, walked to the exit, pushed the door open with a grunt, and disappeared into the rain.

The door banged shut.

Tidwell turned around and walked the aisle to where the man had been sitting. There was nothing there.

He stood, dumfounded.

He wanted desperately to be able to remember every word the man had spoken.

He hurried for the door.

He would ask where the words had come from.

He pushed the door open, the light assaulting his eyes.

But the rainswept parking lot was empty except for Tidwell's car and the other one that had been there before.

Tidwell stood there, frozen, getting pelted by the rain.

It was as if the man had never been there.

25

FRICTION FILLED the air in the squad car as Rickert drove and Brandon rode shotgun. The car had been silent since they'd left the ramshackle trailer where they had confronted Marty Martin, where Nick Tidwell had gotten away, and where they'd exchanged blows.

Brandon's face and neck hurt. He checked his lip again; it had stopped bleeding. He was way too uptight. He knew he needed to settle down. He reviewed the few notes he'd taken in the trailer, got out his cell, and called Detective Ben Briggs. He gave Ben the name of Skip Manford, whom Marty Martin had said owned the trailer they'd just come from. Brandon told Ben he wanted everything he could find on Manford, especially any ties to Sidney Grimaldi.

"Don't you think you should ask me before you do that?" Rickert said, looking straight ahead at the road.

"What was wrong with that?" Brandon said.

"You're the rookie, right? Just run it by me first."

Brandon steamed.

He said no more.

This guy is so puffed up . . . a control freak.

"Got me?" Rickert blurted.

Brandon grunted to give Rickert some form of acknowledgment, but he fumed inside.

After another five minutes of cruising their beat, Rickert mumbled something about how late it was and being starved. He pulled into a Little Caesars and cursed a blue streak because the drive-thru line was so long. He parked the car with a jolt and got out. "You want something, come on." He was gone.

Brandon was starved, too, but believed this was going to be the only opportunity he had to call Deetz, who answered the phone by jesting about the nice visit he'd had from Kristen Trent.

"I don't know where that came from, Dad. We're not that serious," Brandon said, realizing for the first time how bad his jaw hurt. "She didn't even tell me she was planning to go see you."

Deetz laughed it off and said it was a nice visit. He asked something about where Kristen worked, and Brandon interrupted him.

"Dad, Rickert's in Little Caesars right now. I'm in the car. I only have a minute. I need to talk to you."

"Go ahead. What's up?"

"We just came from the residence of the guy I shot yesterday. Two guys were inside. One ran out the back and got away, but I saw him—it was Nick Tidwell."

There was a long pause.

"Are you sure?" Deetz said.

"Yeah. The guy we did catch works as an EMT and admitted he and Nick are work partners."

Brandon quickly explained they found nothing in the mobile home, but he thought the guys may have flushed drugs. He told Deetz he asked Ben Briggs to follow up on Skip Manford. As he explained everything, Brandon was up in the edge of his seat, watching for Rickert to come out of the restaurant.

"There's more. I gotta make this quick," Brandon said. "We ran off two Black kids this morning washing windows at an intersection in Edgewood. They recognized Rickert. When Rickert threatened to take them in, one of them said, 'Go ahead, take us in and I'll tell them what I saw the night at the theater.' The other kid was trying to keep him quiet. Dad, I think we need to find out what that kid knows. He lives in Conklin."

"Hold on, Son. Hold on," Deetz said. "I've got to process this."

Brandon waited anxiously and watched for Rickert.

"What was the guy's name at the house today who said he was Nick's partner?"

"Marty Martin."

"Does Rickert know it was Nick who got away?"

"Yeah. In fact, when I was in another room, Rickert pretty much beat it out of Marty Martin." Brandon didn't have time to tell Deetz about his fight with Rickert; it could wait.

After quite a pause, Deetz said, "I need to tell Tidwell. Has Rickert told anyone yet?"

"I don't think so."

"Did you hear the girl we pulled over yesterday got shot today?"

"What? No!"

"Yeah. She got bail this morning and was shot going into a hotel within an hour."

"Is she dead?"

"Unfortunately, she is."

A flash of anger sparked in Brandon.

"I knew that was going to happen!"

"It was Tidwell's call, ultimately, and he's kicking himself for it now," Deetz said. "I'll call him about Nick. He's gonna lose it. I'll also mention about the other thing. Don't do anything on your own, Brandon. Let's wait and see what Tidwell says."

The door of Little Caesars swung open and Rickert came out holding a pizza box in one hand and a slice of pizza in the other.

"He's coming. I've got to go. The one kid definitely knows something, Dad. He said something about witnesses. Rickert is dirty, I'm telling you."

"Okay, I hear you. Just back off it for now. I'll let you know what Tidwell says."

"Later." Brandon ended the call and scrolled through his phone innocently.

Rickert opened the driver's door. "You want to drive so I can chow?"

Without a word, Brandon got out and they traded places.

Rickert had the box on his lap and a fistful of napkins.

"You didn't want anything in there?" he said with a mouthful.

"Nah, I'm good."

"Suit yourself." Rickert had red sauce on the side of his mouth, which was so full he looked as if he was in the middle of a hot dog eating contest. He opened the box, ripped off another slice, and closed it without offering Brandon any.

Brandon backed up the Interceptor and began heading out of the parking lot.

"Let's go east toward Meridian," Rickert said with a mouthful.

Brandon put his blinker on and Rickert belched so loudly it made Brandon jump.

Rickert thundered with laughter.

Brandon's cheeks burned. His contempt—and disgust—for Harold Rickert increased with each passing minute and he wondered how he'd stand it if he was paired with the man for one more day.

26

Deetz was in a chair in the corner of the bedroom, struggling to get his sweatpants on over the thick bandages on his tender left leg. He paused because he was sweating and out of breath. And the leg hurt badly.

This is not a good idea.

Joanie will be livid.

But, with all that Brandon had told him—about Nick Tidwell and about Harold Rickert's incriminatory run-in with those kids—Deetz felt the need to get dressed and at least see if he could start easing back into work, even if just from home. At the same time he was mentally preparing himself to call Tidwell to relay what Brandon had told him. Deetz's other excuse for getting dressed was that Brandon had sounded so stressed out, Deetz felt he needed to be somewhat mobile, in case he was needed.

This is not smart.

He knew his body needed more rest, more recovery time. He told himself he was just experimenting. And he thought if he could at least get fully dressed and walk out on crutches, Joanie wouldn't think it was so bad.

His phone buzzed, a call, coming from over on the bed about eight to ten feet away. Perhaps this was the incentive he needed.

Deetz took a deep breath, stood with all his weight on his right foot, and pulled up the navy Adidas sweatpants. Breathing hard, he tentatively reached for the crutches that were leaning against the wall and got them positioned in the pits of his arms. They were too short. He had said that to the nurse at the hospital, but she'd ignored him.

I gave you one job.

He started toward the bed. It was taking too long. He wasn't going to get to the phone in time, but that was okay. He was doing it. He was making progress!

"Oh - my - gosh!"

It was Leena. She'd come breezing into the room and stopped suddenly, aghast. "You are so in trouble right now." Her right hand covered her mouth. "Mom is going to have a coronary."

She turned on a dime to leave the room and go tattle on him.

"Honey, stop!" Deetz called. "Come back here. I mean it."

He'd missed the call, but that was now the least of his concerns.

Leena turned around and, reluctantly, came back into the room. She stood there with her arms crossed and her mouth sealed shut with pursed lips.

Deetz realized he looked idiotic. No shirt. Sweatpants. Standing on crutches in the middle of the room. "Don't tell your mom. I'm just seeing how it feels to move around a bit. I have to do this. The doctors don't want me lying in bed all day."

Leena stuck her fists on her waist. "You were told to rest. You were told to take your meds, drink lots of water, and slowly get back on a good diet. You were *not* told to get dressed and walk around the house. That is a complete no."

On the inside, Deetz had to laugh. She was so cute.

"Honey, I'm fine. I'm not going anywhere. Will you please just not say anything to mom? I'll get a shirt on and go out there and she and I will talk about it."

"Do you know what a child you are acting like right now?"

He looked at her and, once again, had to suppress his laughter.

"Yes, I do. But, honey, you know me. I can't sit around here all day and do nothing."

"I'm going to pretend this discussion never happened." Leena turned and went for the door. "Just be warned, Mom is going to literally kill you."

"Leena," Deetz called.

She turned around and opened her eyes wide, listening with a serious glare.

"Grab me a shirt from that second drawer, will you?"

"Are you kidding me right now?" Leena went to the drawer, ripped out the first shirt she found, and tossed it to him on her way back out. He grabbed it while teetering on the crutches.

"Thank you, sweetie. Remember, not a word."

"You made your own bed, now you can lie in it!"

Deetz did laugh this time. What a character she was.

He hobbled to the bed on the crutches, turned around, and sat down with a grunt. He tossed the crutches onto the bed and worked on the shirt Leena had given him, an old gray V-neck T-shirt.

He checked his phone. The missed call was from Tidwell.

Deetz sighed. As a friend, he had to tell Tidwell about Nick; it was going to be another huge blow to the big man. He dialed Tidwell's number and tried to figure out how to break the news.

"Gee, Wayne, I don't know how you could have missed my call," Tidwell answered. "You'd think you'd been shot or something." The hum in the background made it sound like Tidwell was driving.

"Very funny," Deetz said.

"Hey, where in the Bible does it talk about God leading the blind by ways they don't know, and about making rough places smooth, and stuff like that?"

Wow. That one threw Deetz. He wished that's what they could talk about, but the pressing matter was Nick.

"Unfortunately, I'm not a walking Bible. I'll look it up for you and let you know," Deetz said, making a mental note not to forget. "In the meantime, I need to talk to you about something serious."

"Oh, great. You and everybody else . . . Go ahead, hit me."

Deetz told him how Brandon saw Nick running from the supposed drug house and shared everything Brandon had told him.

Deetz could practically hear Tidwell seething through the phone.

There was a long spell of silence.

"Dolby?" Deetz said. "How do you want to handle it?"

Tidwell cursed and chastised Nick. After venting his frustration, he said, "I'll get with him. I'll find out what I can and let you know."

"Dolby, I can't promise Rickert isn't going to blow this up before you can get with Nick," Deetz said.

"I'll call Rickert now and ask him to stand down," Tidwell said. "I'm not beyond doing that."

Deetz then told Tidwell about the run-in Brandon and Rickert had that morning with the boys from Edgewood, and about the one boy's implications that Rickert may have done something dirty the night Lance Burke was shot and killed.

"Doesn't surprise me one bit," Tidwell said. "Listen, Wayne, do you mind if I call Brandon and get the details on that?"

Deetz really didn't want Brandon under any more pressure. "I think I told you everything, Sarge."

"I'm not going to bother him—"

Don't do this.

"He and Rickert are riding together right now," Deetz said.

"Okay, okay." Tidwell's voice tapered off into silence.

Joanie walked in holding a cup of hot tea and stopped dead in her tracks.

All Deetz could do was sit there and stare at her as he held the phone against his face.

"What on earth do you think you're doing?" Joanie said, ignoring the fact that he was on the phone.

Deetz pointed at the phone and whispered, "It's Tidwell."

"I don't care who it is. Why are you dressed?"

"Sounds like you got busted," Tidwell said. "I'll get back to you."

"Okay, good." Deetz ended the call, tossed the phone next to him on the bed, and looked at Joanie.

"Why're you doing this, Wayne? What don't you understand about rest?"

"Brandon needs me, honey. I just can't—"

"Brandon is a grown man. Brandon would think it was *stupid* that you are rushing your recovery."

"Just let me explain what's going on."

"Nothing you can tell me will make this okay." She set the cup on the nightstand hard, spilling it slightly.

"I'm feeling really good, honey. Honestly."

"That's because you've been following the rules—until now." She crossed to the bed—all business—moved his phone and crutches aside, smacked the pillows, and flattened the sheets angrily. "You take those clothes off and get back in this bed, right now."

He began to protest.

"I mean it, Wayne. We're not doing this. You're too old to play Superman. As far as I'm concerned, you can stay home and heal until your retirement. They owe you that."

His official retirement wasn't until December—five more months.

He briefly contemplated arguing his side more but thought better of it. When Joanie was this mad, the smart play was to do exactly what she said—at least for the time being.

27

TIDWELL WAS STARVED—AND needed a drink. As he waited in the drive-thru line at McDonald's, he formulated a crisis management plan. He would contact Brandon first, then Rickert, then Nick.

He got his bag of food (three hamburgers and one chicken sandwich), asked for lots of extra ketchup, and parked around the corner. He opened his door, dumped some of the Coke, closed the door, added a healthy pour of gin, and drank deeply. Gin and Coke wasn't his cocktail of choice, but it beat drinking straight out of the bottle.

He texted Brandon:

> I know you're riding with Rickert but can you get alone and call me? Need to talk for five minutes.

Tidwell opened a hamburger, slathered it with ketchup, and ate ravenously; it was after 3 p.m. He wondered how Janet was doing and thought he should check in on her, but he had a lot of fires to put out first.

Instead of contacting Rickert, he decided to wait a few more minutes on him, thinking Brandon may be able to give him ammunition against Rickert. The gloves might have to come off to protect Nick.

Tidwell dialed Nick's cell phone, fully expecting the call to go straight to voicemail, which it did: "It's Nick. Do your thing." Tidwell didn't bother to leave a message. He ate fast thinking he would drive to Nick's apartment in Hayhurst, about twenty minutes away.

Tidwell's phone buzzed. It was Brandon texting him back:

> Not likely. Can we do it by text? He's driving.

Tidwell took a swig of his drink, contemplated, and composed a text back to Brandon:

> Your dad told me about the boys you met who may know more about the night Lance died and about Rickert's potential involvement. What more can you tell me?

Send.

Tidwell wiped his mouth with the inadequate napkins, wadded up the paper from one hamburger, opened another, and ate. He wasn't even sure Nick still lived at the nurse's place; she'd told Janet she was kicking him out or planning to move herself.

Tidwell's phone sounded. A text from Brandon:

> One of the boys said he recognized Rickert from a theater. I asked what theater and he said Rickert knew what he was talking about. The boy said if we arrested him, he would tell what he had seen that night.

Tidwell re-read the text. Then read it again.

He was dumbfounded.

Lance had been his best friend; they were like brothers. After his murder, Tidwell had done everything in his power to get to the bottom of what had really happened that night. But they never found the weapon that killed Lance. And Rickert had stuck to his story that the shot came from the shadows of the theater entrance.

Tidwell had always wondered. After all, it had been a group of Black teens that Rickert and Lance came upon that night, and Tidwell knew Rickert was racist; everyone knew. Often, Tidwell would whisper to Lance in the heavens and ask, 'What really happened that night, my friend? Where is the person who killed you? Where is the gun? Is Rickert lying? What did he do that night?'

Tidwell stared at the large drink cup for a long moment.

He was ashamed of himself.

Lance wouldn't approve of this—drinking in the afternoon, on the job.

Tidwell was in a daze. He felt dismal. His life was in shambles. He never thought this could happen to him. Yet here he was, a shell of the man he used to be.

"I miss you, Lance," he whispered. "That's about all I know anymore."

Another text came in from Brandon:

> I tried to pursue it but Rickert got loud and forced us out of there. When we were leaving the kid yelled something and I heard the word 'witnesses.' One kid lives in Conklin. That's all I got.

Whoosh. Tidwell's face burned. His head buzzed with static. He had to find that kid. He put all the food and wrappers back in the bag and set it aside. He replied to Brandon's text with a thumbs up, took another swig of his drink, and checked the time.

First, he had to try to keep Nick out of trouble.

And what other motives did he have in doing that? Protecting his own name, of course, which was already tarnished due to his lack of self-control and morning libations.

Tidwell briefly planned what he would say and dialed Harold Rickert. After four rings, Rickert picked up and answered simply by stating his last name.

"Tidwell here."

Tidwell could imagine Rickert looking over at Brandon right then.

"Yes, sir," Rickert said in a smart aleck tone.

"What'd you guys find at that house this morning?" Tidwell baited him.

"Why do I have a feeling you already know?" Rickert said.

"Don't play games, Rickert, just tell me."

"Likely a drug house. Toilet running when we got in. One guy was there, and one ran out back—got away."

Tidwell's chest tightened. He waited.

"It was your boy, Sargent."

Tidwell paused a moment.

"But you have no proof of that," Tidwell said, "and you found no evidence."

"Affirmative," Rickert said. "But the witness we interviewed named your boy. Now you tell me—because you're higher up the food chain than I am—under normal circumstances, we would track down that individual and question him, would we not?"

Tidwell bristled, took a drink, and contemplated how to answer.

"We'll get back to that in a minute. Let's shift gears to Lance Burke," Tidwell said, realizing he was putting Brandon in an awkward position.

Tidwell could hear the hum of the Interceptor and envisioned the sneer Rickert was giving Brandon right about then.

"One of those boys you ran into this morning seemed to have a lot to say about the night Lance was murdered."

"What?" Rickert cussed. "What did you tell him?" He was talking to Brandon. "Look Sarge, those boys were high. And they didn't say nothing about Lance Burke. What is this, your feeble attempt at blackmail?"

"I am going to address this morning's events with my son," Tidwell said. "He will be questioned, by me—"

"Ha." Rickert laughed loudly and mumbled a string of profanity.

"I think we're done," Tidwell said.

"We'll see about that." Rickert ended the call.

28

BRANDON AND RICKERT RODE out the rest of their shift in silence, with tension sizzling between them. Rickert was smoldering because he'd learned Brandon had tipped off Sergeant Tidwell about son Nick fleeing from the drug house. And because Brandon had mentioned the incriminating things those boys had said about Rickert at the intersection in Edgewood that morning.

With a sudden jerk and squeal of the tires, Rickert parked the Interceptor in the parking garage at Bureau headquarters. Brandon couldn't get out fast enough to head for his car to go home. He needed to find out what on earth was up with Kristen and he planned to share with Clarence all that had transpired with Rickert that day.

"Wait just a minute, you little punk," Rickert yelled. He was out of the squad car in a flash, slammed the door, and headed toward Brandon like a bar bouncer going after an underage patron.

Brandon squared up to him, his heart hammering.

"Partners don't pull that crap!" Rickert yelled in Brandon's face with veins bulging from his neck and temples. His dark eyes danced with insanity.

"You're *not* my partner," Brandon said as he turned and walked fast toward his car, trying to get space between himself and the nutcase.

"Come back here!" Rickert called, cussing a blue streak.

Brandon walked faster, thinking Rickert was seriously out of his mind. Getting closer to his car he thought he heard something and turned around—Rickert was in his face.

Brandon shoved him away as hard as he could, like pushing away a rabid animal, not wanting it anywhere near him.

"Get away from me!"

Rickert looked around the parking garage and Brandon was certain the redneck was going to attack him. He was prepared to fight.

Luckily, a male officer and a female officer were heading out the bureau's double-doors, talking and laughing as they walked toward one of the squad cars.

Rickert turned back to Brandon with jaw clenched and nostrils flaring.

"If I so much as hear you *breathe* another word about Lance Burke or that night . . . I will kill you. It's that simple. Do you understand me?"

Brandon was out of breath and his temples pounded. "What did you do?"

"I will break your skinny neck—or slit it—and hide your body where no one will ever find it; not even your over-the-hill old man."

Brandon's stomach dropped like a free-falling elevator. His insides felt as if they had been carved hollow from a mixture of fear and the stark reality that Rickert may really have done something horrible the night Lance Burke died.

Brandon backed away and moved toward his car, checking back to keep an eye on the crazed officer.

"That's right, you better go," Rickert yelled. "Go home to mommy and daddy. Just remember what I told you. I won't hesitate to end you."

Rickert suddenly took a giant step toward Brandon, which echoed loudly, faking that he was coming. Brandon jumped with surprise and Rickert roared with laughter.

"You better hope you don't get paired up with me again," Rickert said, looking around. The cops who'd been walking were now backing out of their spot with their windows up. "I'll make your life complete misery."

134

Brandon knew better than to say a word. He got in his car, trembling, locked the doors, and backed out of his spot fast.

This guy is completely nuts.

The other cops were exiting the parking deck and Rickert was now yelling at Brandon through the car windows.

"Remember what I told you!"

Brandon's tires squealed as he patched out and whizzed past Rickert, who was glaring at him the whole way, yelling, and making slashing motions across his throat in warning.

BRANDON WAS TREMBLING and lightheaded in the moments after his run-in with Rickert. During his drive home, he called Deetz and told him about the fiasco with Rickert, which, he complained, was caused by Sergeant Tidwell's interference.

"Tidwell pushed me, so I told him about those kids in Edgewood, and the next thing I know Rickert is all over me about it. That guy's a psycho, Dad."

"What a mess," Deetz said. "I'm sorry that happened, Son. I'm afraid Sergeant Tidwell is going through some heavy stuff right now —personally and professionally."

"I just hope Rickert and I aren't assigned to ride together again."

"You won't be. I'll tell Tidwell—"

"No, Dad. I'll tell him. It's my problem. I need to talk to him anyway. We need to find those boys and find out what they know about the night Lance died—"

"Brandon, listen to me. You let Tidwell handle that. That's in his court now. After what happened with you and Rickert today, you need to stay out of it. Do you understand me?"

Brandon wasn't going to argue with his dad, especially because he didn't want him to get all bent out of shape while he was trying to recover, but Brandon wasn't going to let this thing go. He detested Rickert and was intent on learning the truth about what happened the night Lance Burke died.

"Did you hear me, Son?"

"Yeah."

"Yeah, what?" Deetz said.

"Dad, I need to tell Clarence about this. He has to ride with Rickert. He needs to know what's going on."

Deetz sighed in frustration.

"He won't tell anyone. I'll make sure of it," Brandon said, certain that he was pushing his dad's blood pressure through the roof.

"Son, listen to me. This job is stressful enough without all this drama."

"Dad! Rickert threatened to kill me. This isn't some little, friendly argument. He's covering up what happened that night. We need to jump on this, now."

"Call Tidwell!" Deetz blurted. "He needs to handle this. I'll call him—"

"Dad, no! You don't need to be getting all worked up about this. Please. You need to rest and recover. I've got this. *You* need to trust *me* for once. It's your turn to have some faith."

29

TIDWELL HIT a patch of late afternoon rush hour traffic on his way to Hayhurst but welcomed it because it gave him a chance to add a splash more gin to his watered-down Coke. By the time he got to Nick's neighborhood, he was feeling buoyant and was confident he would catch Nick before his night shift. It was constant maintenance with this kid and Tidwell wondered if Nick would ever get his act together.

He swung the Charger into the shady parking lot at the Bay Breeze apartment complex and cruised around until he found Nick's beat up Ford Ranger pickup truck.

Good.

Tidwell's phone vibrated. He parked, turned off the car, and looked at the screen. A text from Deetz:

> I think that scripture is from Isaiah 42:16: 'I will lead the blind by ways they have not known, along unfamiliar paths I will guide them; I will turn the darkness into light before them and make the rough places smooth. These are the things I will do; I will not forsake them.'

Tidwell nodded, smiled, and sighed as he looked around at the tall trees whose leaves danced pleasantly in the evening breeze.

Leave it to Deetz to remember.

CRESTON MAPES

That's what Deetz did; he thought about other people.

What a concept.

Tidwell lit up his phone and re-read the text slowly, digesting each word. When he was finished, he dropped the phone and whispered, "I need you to do that—because I'm blind." He looked over at the bottle of gin. "A stupid fool."

What a mess.

He found Nick's apartment number on his phone, checked himself in the rearview mirror—eyes small and sunken, lines everywhere—and opened the door to head in.

Once on his feet, he realized he was more buzzed than he'd anticipated.

As he avoided puddles from the earlier rain, his steps felt awkwardly long and he was a bit off balance.

What would it mean for him to be led along unfamiliar paths?

Would Nick tell him the truth about running from that house this morning, or would he pretend he hadn't been there?

Maybe he hadn't been there. Maybe this was all a mistake.

Tidwell checked the signs with the apartment numbers and figured Nick's place was four doors down.

His phone buzzed, a call this time.

He got it out and looked.

Janet.

His first thought was, is she okay? Was it her head?

He stopped, turned, and walked toward a well-manicured courtyard area where there were several wet benches and a small pond with a bridge.

"Hello."

"Dolby, it's me," Janet said.

"Hey, everything okay?"

"Yes. I'm, uh, I've had a good day. Feeling better."

"That's good. What's going on?"

"Where are you?"

"I'm actually at Nick's place—about to go to the door."

"Oh . . ." Concern arose in her voice.

"He was spotted by police this morning, running from a possible drug house. He wasn't caught, but someone recognized him. I'm going to find out what's going on."

138

"Oh dear . . . where? Where was this?"

"Edgewood. Bad part of town."

"What do you mean a 'possible drug house?'"

Tidwell had been staring into the pond's green water in a daze and suddenly looked around toward Nick's door. He didn't want to miss him.

"It involves the people who shot Deetz. Possible ties to Sidney Grimaldi. It's serious."

"Oh, Dolby . . ."

"I know. Let me go. I need to see him before he goes to work."

"Okay. Uh—"

"What else?" he said, realizing he sounded impatient.

"Look . . . I'm meeting Greg Stovall for a cup of coffee—in an hour."

She blurted it out, set it out there like placing a bomb right at his feet in a nicely wrapped package.

Tidwell spun around and stalked toward the bridge, not believing her audacity. "Oh, so now you're going to come out and tell me instead of hiding it? What are you saying, Janet? What's going on?"

Tidwell's temples pounded and he walked up onto the bridge.

"It's a cup of coffee. Out in public. Just to talk."

"With another man! This is insane. Why are you doing this? We haven't even been to counseling—"

"Dolby, I'm not going to live like we've been living."

"We're married, Janet! You don't go meet another guy for coffee. I'm gonna kill that guy; you tell him that for me."

"Dolby, we are on a road to nowhere. To no good. Things have got to change—"

"Okay, they'll change, but that doesn't involve another man. You are sick, Janet. What if I did that?"

Silence.

Then, finally she said, "This is something I want to do and I'm not going to hide it from you. Life's too short. I could have been killed in that wreck. I'm not going to . . . waste my life away."

Tidwell bit his tongue and shook his head to try to clear it, wishing he was sober.

This was not Janet. This was not what a devoted wife did. This was not the kind of person she was.

"This is bad, Janet."

"That's what I've been trying to tell you, Dolby." She cussed.

"Meeting him is going to make it worse."

There was a long pause.

"How long am I supposed to keep going like this? Nothing ever changes. I'm not going to live my life like this."

"You need to give it a chance—"

"What do you think I've been doing for the past year—more than a year?"

"It's all about you, isn't it?"

"Listen to you! Who's the one married to his job? Who's the one married to his booze? Who's the one that's . . . that's discarded his wife like a pair of old shoes? You're the selfish one here. All you do is think about yourself."

Tidwell's head spun. He was furious. But he was also befuddled. Her words hurt him. Frustrated him. Silenced him.

"Let's be done with this," she finally said. "Give Nick my love. Let me know what happens."

There was a pause.

Tidwell was overcome with despair.

He was about to change the topic back to Nick, but Janet ended the call.

30

BRANDON WAS PHYSICALLY and mentally drained by the time he buzzed his way into the fourth-floor apartment he shared with rookie Portland cop Clarence Waters. As usual, Brandon was hit by the strong aroma of some type of rice or tofu or spicy Caribbean whatever.

"Let me guess," Brandon called to the kitchen as he tossed his backpack on the couch. "Sausage and mango."

"Try again," Clarence yelled.

Brandon rounded the corner to the small kitchen, which was filled mostly by Clarence's massive six-foot-three-inch frame. But he stopped in his tracks when he saw Kristen, throwing her arms into the air, yelling, "Surprise!"

Brandon's face burned.

Talk about awkward.

She was showing up everywhere, unannounced.

And Brandon was in no mood for it.

"I expected more of a welcome than that," Kristen whined, with her hands now stabbed at her waist.

Brandon managed a smile, put his hands atop her shoulders, and gave her a peck on the cheek. "What are you doing here?"

"This gets better by the second," she complained.

Clarence glanced at Brandon, flashed his eyes open wide and raise his eyebrows, as if to say, 'Wow, this has been weird."

Kristen swung around and grabbed a big glass of white wine from the counter and offered it to Brandon.

"No thanks." Brandon was frustrated she was there. He needed to wind down and talk to Clarence. He peered around the big man toward the stove and said, "Mmm, that looks amazing."

"Clarence's city chicken on dirty rice with my special Cajun seasoning."

"And I'm invited to stay," Kristen said, smiling, and swinging her shoulders from one side to the other.

This irritated Brandon and he realized he had to say something.

"What do you want to drink, honey?" she said.

Brandon looked around. Clarence was also having a glass of white wine.

"Nothing right now. I've got to change clothes." He looked at Kristen and said softly, "Can we talk a minute?"

Her happy countenance instantly deflated.

Clarence kept himself busy humming at the stove but shot Brandon a humorous look of fright.

Brandon led the way into the living room and Kristen followed him.

He turned to face her, and she set down her wine glass, hugged him, and said, "I'm so glad to see you."

He pulled away slightly, held her at the elbows, looked her in the eyes, and said, "We need to talk."

She blinked, tilted her head, and squinted. "What about?"

"Let's sit." Brandon plunked down on the couch and patted the seat next to him.

But Kristen only stood there. "What do we need to talk about?"

"Sit down."

"No. What is it?"

Brandon stood, walked around the coffee table, and approached her—feeling like a trainer with a wild animal.

Kristen backed up several steps.

"Okay, look . . . I had a really rough day," Brandon said. "On days like this, I need some down time to clear my head . . . I just wasn't expecting you to be here—"

She started to protest but he was determined to finish saying what he needed to say. "We didn't make plans—for you to come over."

"We said we were having dinner tonight!" she said.

"No. We didn't! You ended your phone message saying, 'How about dinner,' but I never even responded to that."

"That's not how it went. We agreed we were meeting for dinner. If you didn't want to, you should have called me and told me."

Brandon shook his head. "You suggested, I didn't respond. I can show you the text. Kristen, I don't like this . . . this . . ." He wanted to say he didn't like being forced to be with her, but he knew if he did, she would blow a gasket.

"What don't you like?" Kristen said in an angry tone. "Spit it out. I'm a big girl."

"Just . . . showing up unannounced. I . . . I'm not down for that."

There.

I said it.

It took only a split-second for the fallout.

Kristen whirled around, stalked off, grabbed her purse, and charged back toward Brandon.

"I'll tell you what. I won't show up unannounced, or any other way! Maybe you'll be happy with that."

"Kris, just wait a minute. Don't do this."

She blew across the room and out the door without another word.

After the door slammed shut there was a moment of silence. Clarence leaned out of the kitchen with his apron on, staring at Brandon wide-eyed with his mouth gaping. "Boy, you did it this time."

"Dude, we didn't have plans tonight."

"She said you did."

"She lied! This has gotten really weird, really fast."

"Come on, man, sit down, have some city chicken. We'll talk about it."

"Let me change real quick. It'll take me less than five minutes."

. . .

BRANDON AND CLARENCE ate at the small table in the kitchen over some of the best food Brandon had ever eaten. He filled Clarence in on all the details about Kristen's strange behavior of late, and then the conversation turned to his vexing day partnering with Harold Rickert.

After they both got a second helping of rice and chicken, Brandon told Clarence everything—about seeing Tidwell's son dash from the drug house; about how Rickert beat Marty Martin until he named Nick Tidwell; about fighting with Rickert in the drug house; about the run-in with the Black kids that morning, who knew something about the night Lance Burke died; and even about the bite mark on Rickert's ear and the autopsy report that stated that the bullet that killed Lance Burke had come from closer than Rickert had said.

Clarence shoved his plate away, backed his chair up several feet from the table, and clasped his large hands behind his head with a huff. "I knew it!" he said. "That guy's dirty as the day is long. So he killed that cop . . ." He pulled his chair back up and leaned his strong arms on the table, glaring at Brandon with his large brown eyes, the whites of which were brilliant white.

"You've got to keep all this between us," Brandon said. "I promised my dad—"

"This guy should not only not be a cop, he should be in jail."

"I need to find those boys, especially the one who wanted to talk. The other one was trying to keep him quiet."

"I'll go with you."

Brandon shrugged. "We'd never find them."

"You don't know that. You said they were out washing windows at stop lights. It's worth a try."

"My dad told me to let Tidwell handle it."

"Dude, from what I can tell, Tidwell has his own problems. It can't hurt for us to drive out there."

"Now?"

"You got somewhere else you need to be?"

31

TIDWELL WAS SO furious he almost fired his phone into the pond outside Nick's apartment but stopped himself. He stood there for a long time, silent, with his hands on his waist, thinking a million thoughts about the good times he and Janet had shared in the past, and that this must be what it felt like to be on the brink of divorce.

Divorce!

Never ever had it entered Tidwell's mind that he and Janet would not be together. They had that strong of a relationship. A true bond.

For the first time he wondered if she might be on drugs or something—to come out and say she was meeting another man for coffee!

Or could Tidwell's own behavior be so rotten it had driven her to this?

He couldn't fathom it.

The big man huffed and turned back toward Nick's apartment.

Now he had to face this debacle.

And he didn't have much patience left. Nick was twenty-four years old, for crying out loud. A man. And here Tidwell was, still propping him up. That's what parents did today. He'd read an article recently that stated seventy percent of parents support their adult children financially into their late twenties.

Unbelievable.

Not me!

As he got to the sidewalk and approached the apartment, Tidwell determined he would dump the Coke and put straight gin in the cup for the ride home. It had been that kind of day.

He knocked at the door and waited. The shades were drawn and there was condensation on the windows.

If this was the 'unfamiliar path' God was talking about in that scripture, Tidwell wanted nothing to do with it.

He heard footsteps approach the door. Then there was a pause and Tidwell imagined Nick was looking through the peephole at him.

A chain rattled, then the bolt lock clicked loudly, then the door slowly opened about six inches. It was dark inside. Tidwell looked down at the young lady who was Nick's roommate.

She only looked up at him with her small mouth sealed shut, and her shiny brown eyes blinking.

"Hey, you must be Jody," Tidwell said. "I'm Nick's dad. Is he home?"

She looked down at her bare feet. She wore denim cutoffs and a short-sleeved sweatshirt featuring artwork of a black Labrador retriever. She looked back up at him, blinked slowly, and spoke quietly. "He's sleeping—before his shift."

Tidwell lowered his voice. "I really need to see him. Can I come in?"

Jody stared up at Tidwell with sad eyes and a blank gaze. She was a pretty young lady, with freckles on her nose and cheeks. With a sigh, she turned around and walked away leaving the door ajar.

Tidwell paused briefly, pushed the door open, and walked inside. It was cold. He stopped so his eyes could adjust to the dark. The shades were all closed and backlit from the outside light of evening. Ceiling fans were on and the AC was cranked.

"You want anything?" Jody said from the small kitchen, lit only by the dim light above the stove. "Tea. Coffee. Water."

"No. Thanks." Tidwell stepped farther in. There was a large gray sectional couch and a big TV on the wall. It was turned off. Books, magazines, video games and controllers, and a pack of cigarettes and lighter were strewn on a large, square coffee table. There wasn't much else in the place, except a narrow bookcase on the far wall with several framed photos that Tidwell couldn't make out from where he was standing.

"You want me to wake him up?" she said.

For the first time, Tidwell noticed a large bruise on Jody's left bicep. Their eyes met. She glanced down at the bruise and immediately turned away.

"What time is he due at work?" Tidwell said.

"Seven."

Tidwell checked the time: 6:20 p.m.

"I do. This is really important."

Jody crossed her arms and took several steps toward Tidwell. "Just so you know, he needs to be out by tomorrow night."

Tidwell examined the serious look on her face. "I see," he said. "Do you mind me asking why he's leaving? What's going on?"

She blinked slowly and sighed. "He's messed up. High all the time. I think he's dealing."

"High on what?"

"Crack. Booze. Whatever he can get his hands on."

"Dealing what?"

"Don't know, don't care. Just want him gone."

It dawned on Tidwell that Nick was, in a way, following in his footsteps.

Jody walked toward a small hallway and stopped just before. She turned to Tidwell and held up the arm with the bruise. Showed it to him. Then held up her right wrist. It was also badly bruised.

"He did this."

Tidwell could only stare with his mouth gaping.

His temperature ascended like an infrared gravity convection oven.

There was no way.

Shame engulfed him like a gas-lit bonfire.

His face fell with sorrow and embarrassment.

He stepped toward her with an outstretched arm, starting to say how sorry he was.

She shook her head and pulled away like a streetwise kid who'd been beat too much.

"Just get him out. And make sure he never comes back."

She pointed at the first door on the right. "He's in there."

She disappeared into the room on the left and shut the door quietly.

Tidwell stared at the door behind which his son was sleeping.

He clenched his teeth, took a deep breath, and sighed.

Then he went in with both barrels loaded.

THE BEDROOM WAS DARK. Tidwell knew Nick had the blackout shades, because he often slept during the day and worked at night. The nasty smell in the room was a mixture of marijuana, cigarettes, and some other sour odor, possibly dirty clothes, or spilled beer.

Tidwell turned on the flashlight on his phone and shone the bluish white light across the room.

What he saw made him sick—and angry.

The king size bed was covered in a mess of clothes and sheets and dark blankets; Nick was somewhere underneath. A tall green bong sat on the nightstand next to a clock, cigarettes, a box of tissue, and a light with a crooked lampshade. A large, empty suitcase was open on the floor. There was a trashcan in the corner overflowing with fast food wrappers, beer cans, and empty booze bottles. Clothes, towels, shoes, and trash were strewn everywhere.

Tidwell's stomach ached.

He found a lamp on a dresser and turned it on. He put his phone in his pocket. The light didn't budge Nick.

Tidwell crossed to the bed and pulled the blankets back until he found Nick's head. He shook one of his shoulders. "Nick, wake up. It's Dad." He repeated the process until his son opened his eyes and squinted up at the tall figure.

"Dad?" Nick patted around until he found his phone. It lit up and he looked at the time. He grunted and sat up.

"Why does that young lady have bruises?" Tidwell said.

Nick rubbed his face and started to sit up, but Tidwell gritted his teeth and shoved him back down as hard as he could.

Nick just stayed there like a rag doll that had been tossed, which infuriated Tidwell even more.

"I can't do this right now," Nick moaned. "I've got to be at work."

Tidwell put a knee on the soft bed, leaned over his son, and shook him. "How dare you hurt a woman!"

"Dad—"

"Shut up, Nick. Just shut your face."

Nick's head flopped down on the bed and his whole body settled.

"You're going to be out of here by tomorrow. Right?"

"Why are you here?"

"Shut up! Shut up, Nick. You were seen running from a drug house in Edgewood this morning. Why were you there?"

"What? Dad, listen—"

"No! You listen." Tidwell grabbed Nick and yanked him to the edge of the bed, straining and hurting his own back in the process. "You're going to tell me the truth right now. Tell me!"

Nick began to rise, and Tidwell yelled "Tell me" and shoved him hard back down on the bed.

"I'm in trouble," Nick said. "In debt. Me and my partner . . . we started selling drugs—to pay back the money."

"What kind of drugs?"

"Ice . . . crystal meth."

Tidwell had to restrain himself from slapping Nick.

"Where're you getting it?"

"We . . . we've gotten in with some bad people, Dad. I'm sorry. I'm . . . I know this is, I know I'm not—"

"What bad people? Sidney Grimaldi? Talk!"

"I've heard it's Grimaldi, but I've never seen him. We think that's a rumor. We don't know. No one knows."

"Who are you selling to?"

"People on our beat."

"What beat? During work? You're selling meth out of your ambulance?"

"We make one stop—in the middle of the night. No one—"

"What are you on, besides booze and pot?"

Nick buried his head in the pillows.

Tidwell shook him. "Answer me!"

"Leave me alone! I'm an adult." Nick jerked aways and sat up angrily on the edge of the bed. No shirt. Skinny. All bones.

"How much do you owe? To whom?"

Nick got to his feet. He wore black boxers. His size thirteen feet were narrow and bony. He crossed unsteadily to a bathroom. He turned around to face Tidwell and leaned against the doorframe.

"I owe Jody three month's rent. Whoever the drugs are coming from, I owe them like eight grand. If I stop selling, they'll kill me. Is that all? I gotta get to work." Nick forged into the bathroom, flicked on the lights, and groaned.

"Give me a name. Who you answer to when selling the drugs."

"No, Dad. I can't."

"Just one name, so I can look into it."

Nick began to protest and Tidwell fired back at him. "This is for you, to help you! My gosh, are you so blind, Son? Why would I want a name, other than to help you?"

"Maybe to make a big bust so you can keep climbing the ladder."

"What the—"

"LaRocca." Nick held up his hands to stop Tidwell from saying any more. "LaRocca. That's all I got."

Tidwell just stood there, so mad, so broken, so weary.

Has Nick even thought about where he's going to move tomorrow? Did he just assume he could move home? When was he going to say anything? Or maybe he planned to stay with Jody, against her wishes.

Tidwell left the room and knocked on the door of the room Jody had entered. When she came to the door, he asked her to write down the amount Nick owed, and her exact mailing address; he would send a check. She did so and gave it to Tidwell, who slipped it in his pocket and headed toward Nick's room.

"Mr. Tidwell," Jody said softly.

He stopped and turned around.

"He's got to get to a point where he wants help. He doesn't right now. Everyone enables him. I did and you are. He needs to be allowed to fail. He needs to grow up."

Her door shut and Tidwell stood there and let that soak in.

He headed back into Nick's room and found him leaning over the bathroom sink, shaving.

"Where were you planning to go tomorrow?" Tidwell said.

Nick stopped shaving and turned to face his dad. "Can I come home?"

He'd just assumed he could show up on their doorstep.

Pitiful.

Tidwell and Janet had planned to paint and update Nick's bedroom, turn it into a guest room, and now he would be staying there, indefinitely.

"Just till I get my feet back on the ground." He finished shaving, rinsed, and tapped the razor.

Tidwell was incensed. He was being forced to decide between letting Nick fail and providing him enough rope not to hang himself.

"If we say yes there are *no* drugs," Tidwell said, coldly. "If that means going to those meetings, you go. And you get out of debt."

Nick rinsed his face, patted his cheeks with the towel on his shoulder, looked at his dad in the mirror, and smiled. "That's the plan."

32

CLARENCE DROVE and Brandon rode shotgun along I-84 toward Portland's east side. Rush hour had passed and the sun was setting with brilliant orange and blue hues. They had the windows down in the red 2015 Chevy Malibu and Brandon was filling Clarence in on the day's events in more detail.

As they exited the interstate and headed into Bridgepark, Brandon got a call from his dad. He put it on speaker.

"I've been talking with Sid at headquarters," Deetz said. "They found the red Golf that shot at us—in Prairie Town. It was stripped, bleached, and burned. No prints. No nothing."

Brandon and Clarence glanced at each other, realizing they were dealing with serious pros.

"I talked to Tidwell about those kids you and Rickert ran into," Deetz continued. "He's going to have you drive back out there tomorrow."

"Who's he partnering me with?" Brandon said, looking at Clarence.

"It sounds like Sullivan. You know him?"

"Yeah. Big guy. Gray hair?"

"Yep. He's good police. Tidwell didn't tell him anything about the boys, of course, but he's going to have you back out in that same area. If you see them, get their contact info, numbers, addresses, whatever you can. Tidwell wants to talk to them himself."

Clarence pointed for Brandon to show him which way to go. Brandon did so and Clarence turned the Malibu in the direction of where Brandon had seen the boys earlier that day.

"Mr. Deetz, this is Clarence. I hate to ask, sir, but does this mean I'm back with Rickert?" He shot Brandon a worried look.

There was a pause. "I'm afraid so, Clarence."

"Oh, great. You made my night."

"Hang in there, big guy. It won't be long till your training is done. Then you move on. In the meantime, my advice is to try to keep your mouth shut and mind your own business. Ride it out. It'll be over soon."

"Easier said than done with that psycho," Brandon said, pointing for Clarence to hang a left.

"Brandon, that's not necessary, Son. Just be patient and keep your mouth shut, too. If anything's to come of this, Tidwell will handle it."

Brandon and Clarence looked at each other as if on eggshells.

"Where are you guys headed?" Deetz said.

Clarence shook his head vehemently at Brandon, showing him clearly that he wasn't going to touch that question with a ten-foot pole.

"Uh, just . . . out for a cruise," Brandon said, then waited on pins and needles, knowing it was a lame answer.

"Not seeing Kristen tonight?"

"Oh, uh, she was over for a bit."

Deetz could access Brandon's location on the Find My Friends app. They had it hooked up simply because Brandon was a cop and Deetz wanted to be able to know where he was in case of an emergency. But Deetz did not spy on Brandon. His mom would be more likely to do that than Deetz, and even she didn't make a habit of keeping a close eye on his location.

"How are you feeling, Mr. Deetz?" Clarence changed the subject and Brandon gave him a smile and a thumbs up.

"Not bad, Clarence. Thank you. I was up and about on the crutches for a bit a little while ago. Mrs. Deetz doesn't like it. I'm not a good patient. I'm itching to get back to work."

They wrapped up the call.

"We already passed the intersection we saw them at," Brandon said. "Let's head toward Conklin. You know how to go?"

"Not unless I pull it up on my phone," Clarence said.

"No need. Just take this right up here. I'm getting to know this place pretty well."

"I see that . . . some of this looks pretty sketchy."

The road was riddled with potholes and uneven, broken sidewalks. The houses were tiny and unkempt, most with old metal roofs and peeling paint. Poor looking kids flew by on bicycles. Men sat in rusty chairs along the street, smoking and laughing. Women talked with their hair up in curls and towels, wearing slippers, and cutoff jeans.

"Lots of drugs," Brandon said.

"What do they do for work?"

Brandon shrugged. "Not many people in Conklin work. Government subsidized. There's government housing a couple blocks over."

"Sad."

"My dad says there's a couple sections in Bridgepark where a good number of the people work in machinery, manufacturing, that sort of thing."

They rode in silence, scanning the neighborhood for the boys Brandon had seen that morning.

"What about them?" Clarence pointed to a group of kids hanging out on the corner of Weston and Parks.

"Nope, but that's the right age," Brandon said. "Take a right here."

They cruised in silence and Brandon noticed Clarence checking and rechecking his rearview mirror.

"What do you see back there?" Brandon said.

"I hope I'm wrong."

Brandon turned around and looked out the back window. Some fifty yards back was a dark compact car that resembled Kristen's Kia Forte.

"Is that her?" Clarence said.

Brandon turned back around to face the front with a grunt, got his phone, and checked Find My Friends—but Kristen had disabled her location, so he couldn't tell if that was her car behind them. But he had an awful feeling it was.

"I'm not believing this." Brandon looked straight ahead, embarrassed and trying to figure out what to do if that was her.

"This is getting weirder by the minute," Brandon said.

Clarence had slowed down some and glanced in the mirror again. "Dude, that's her. What do you want to do?"

Brandon's temper flared. "Pull over."

Clarence did so quickly, swerving to the right curb and stopping the Malibu. He and Brandon swiveled around at the same time to watch the Forte. As it got closer, Brandon could make out Kristen driving the car. He was stunned.

Her car approached slowly.

"That's her," Clarence said. "What is she doing?"

The Forte slowed down and eased right up alongside Clarence's car and came to a stop.

Her window that was closest to them went down.

Brandon and Clarence looked at her in silence.

"Now this is what I call a coincidence," Kristen said. "What are you guys doing over here?"

Clarence looked at Brandon, obviously wanting him to say something.

"What are you doing, Kris?" Brandon called.

"I'll ask you the same question, Brandon." She spoke in a snarky, offensive tone.

"Why are you following us?" Brandon said, still in disbelief.

Kristen laughed. "You give yourself too much credit. I've got my reasons for being over here. What about you?"

Clarence looked at Brandon with an expression of awkwardness and they both shook their heads and sighed.

A car pulled up behind Kristen, stopped, and honked.

Brandon was miffed, yet he felt sorry for Kristen.

"Pull over, Kris," he yelled.

She pulled forward and parked in front of Clarence, at a bad angle along the curb.

"Give me five minutes," Brandon whispered to Clarence and got out of the car.

"Good luck, dude, you're gonna need it," Clarence said.

Brandon jogged up to Kristen's car, got in the front passenger seat, and stared at her, unsure what to say.

She reached over and grabbed his hand. "I don't want to lose you."

He squeezed her hand and looked intently into her somewhat frantic eyes. He believed at that moment, more than ever, that she needed the help of a professional counselor. "We need to plan to sit down and talk. Really talk."

"About what? You're going to dump me, aren't you?" she said.

"About us. About you. About me. We need to get everything out on the table."

"I'm not hiding anything from you, Brandon. I swear."

He nodded and patted her hand. "Okay. When can we talk? What about tomorrow after work? We can meet somewhere private." He would tell her then that he wanted her to seek the help of a counselor.

"You're going to dump me; I know you are."

"Kris, let's just take the next step—"

"No! Tell me, right here, right now, that you don't want to end our relationship."

Brandon couldn't tell her that. She was being nuts. She needed help from a professional, that's all he knew.

"See! You can't say it!"

"Kris, this is not the time or place—"

She hit him hard on the arm and did so again and again.

He pulled back and insisted she stop.

"I won't let you dump me. You owe me. You—"

Beyond Kristen, out the window of her car, Brandon spotted the two Black boys for whom they'd been searching. They were riding their bikes along the sidewalk with heavy plastic bags hanging from their handlebars.

"That's who we're looking for. I've got to go." Brandon threw the door open to Kristen's wide eyes and protests. "We'll talk tomorrow."

He waved to Clarence that those were the boys, ran back to the Malibu, and jumped in.

They roared off leaving Kristen in tears.

33

TIDWELL WAS FEELING no pain by the time he got home. After the blowout with Nick, straight gin in the Coke cup on the drive back had been a necessity. He'd planned to go break up Janet's little rendezvous with Greg Stovall, but she'd turned off her location on Find My Friends.

Probably for the best . . . I may've killed the guy.

Feeling a bit fuzzy and as if he was gliding on air, Tidwell grabbed his favorite beer in its amber-colored bottle, a bag of pretzels, and his laptop, let Lady out, and plunked down in his favorite chair on the front porch. It was a cool night with little breeze and the small accent lights along the border of the lawn reflected dew on the grass. Lady had picked up a scent and was zig-zagging every which way.

Janet was still out.

Tidwell drank and munched pretzels, staring out over the front lawn and thinking about the AA meeting he'd been to that morning, which seemed like days ago. That little Neil Houser fellow had tried to help him. Those people were finding a solution to their problem.

Good for them.

It crossed Tidwell's mind that he was on the precipice of . . . something. He knew things couldn't go on as they were. It felt as if things were going to get dramatically better or drastically worse. As it was, everything was a mess, in limbo. Nick's life. His marriage. Yet, God was being patient with him.

Sid and Angie had cut him slack that morning.

The Englishman at the church, Farnsworth, had entered his life unexpectedly and with great drama. Tidwell pictured the man's large, clear eyes and recalled how he said he never drove down that road; how he'd seen the bottle of gin in Tidwell's car; how God had instructed him to go into the church; how he'd emotionally recited the scripture, then vanished into the rain.

"I will lead the blind by ways they have not known."

That would mean change.

Lady wandered into the woods.

"Hey, come," he called. "Come, Lady."

She turned around and trotted back into the yard.

"Good girl."

Perhaps tomorrow he would stop drinking for a few days. Clear his head. Detox his body. He had planned on doing that often and never followed through with it. His excuse was that he enjoyed alcohol. Deserved it after a long day of work. It relaxed him. Besides, everyone drank. The same old story. Same old excuses.

Lady chased her tail.

Crickets chirped.

He examined the stars in the clear indigo sky and his head spun slightly.

Where is Janet?

The thought of her meeting that guy infuriated him and if he dwelled on it more than a few seconds, he would go ballistic. In the past, in good times, she would have texted to let him know where she was and when she would be home. *Not anymore.*

His thoughts turned with melancholy to Lance Burke and what Brandon Deetz had told him about those boys he'd met and the fact that they may have more information about the night Lance died.

Perhaps Tidwell would have Brandon ride out to Conklin with him to try to find the boys and learn exactly what they knew. Tidwell had always had the feeling Harold Rickert wasn't telling the complete truth. And, with all those Black kids there that night, and Rickert's passion for prejudice, who knew what may have really gone down.

"I'm going to find out, Lance," Tidwell whispered up toward the stars.

Lady wandered over and up the steps.

"Want a treat?" Tidwell tossed her a pretzel. She ate it, came over, and laid down next to him.

Tomorrow he would send Jody a check for Nick's past due rent.

What about the eight grand he owed?

Tidwell remembered the man Nick had mentioned, LaRocca. He drained the beer and set it aside along with the pretzels and opened his laptop. Once online, he logged into LEDS—Oregon's police database—and searched LaRocca's name.

What kept nagging at Tidwell was the fact that Brandon and Rickert were aware that Nick had run from the drug house.

Nick is dealing. He should be arrested.

If anyone else found out Tidwell was covering for Nick, protecting him from questioning, shielding him from the law— Tidwell would be fired on the spot.

As Tidwell had suspected, there weren't many LaRoccas in the database, and one immediately caught his interest: Antonio D. LaRocca (nickname D-Love). Born in 1965. From Cleveland, Ohio. Did time in Steubenville State Penitentiary for forfeiting, racketeering, and money laundering. Did time in Mansfield Rehabilitation Center for drug trafficking (fentanyl). Moved to Portland in 2017.

Tidwell examined D-Love's mugshot. He was a grizzly, rogue-looking character with a smashed nose, a vertical scar on his wide forehead, and one black eyebrow higher than the other. He was smiling in the photo, revealing a missing tooth way off to one side. A side-note stated he was the first cousin of Sidney Grimaldi, one of Portland's all-time top drug offenders.

Tidwell sat there, staring at the mugshot, the wheels in his mind turning. He could go to this guy, offer to pay what Nick owed, in cash, and request that Nick be removed from the drug operation.

But these were the people who shot Wayne Deetz, who killed that Deborah girl when she was released on bond. Nick was tied up with them!

Tidwell's face got hot. He picked up the bottle of beer to drink, realized it was empty, and cussed. Automatically, he went into the house, got another beer, and returned to his seat on the porch. Lady never moved. No word from Janet.

He examined D-Love's page again and found an address, which he didn't recognize. He searched it on his phone. The red pin landed in a neighborhood several miles from the drug house where Nick was seen leaving. It was a much nicer part of Portland, called Canton Falls. Some high-end homes over that way.

Tidwell bent over and stroked Lady's soft head and ears; she raised up slightly, glanced at him, then put her head back down at a crooked angle against the leg of Tidwell's chair. He wondered if he should tell Deetz what he was thinking of doing—with D-Love.

Deetz would say no way. He would hate the idea. Why? Because Tidwell would be jeopardizing his own career and reputation for Nick—who was guilty of dealing drugs.

Maybe Deetz would have a better plan.

Tidwell looked at the time: 9:28 p.m. Too late to call, but not too late to text to see if Deetz was still up.

He was almost finished composing a text to Deetz—telling him about Nick's involvement with D-Love and his idea to pay Nick's debt to get him out of the Grimaldi operation—when he heard a car.

Janet.

The headlights came up the driveway, flooded the trees, and, yes, it was Janet—in the rental car the insurance company had lined up for her, a little gray SUV.

Tidwell sent the text to Deetz and sat there in the dark.

Janet stopped the car next to the Charger, the headlights went off, and the car turned off. Janet's phone lit up in front of her and it looked as if she was texting someone. Tidwell didn't think she saw him sitting there.

Finally, her door opened and Janet slowly emerged from the car. She stood a bit askew with her high heels in the gravel, situated the sling on her arm, took a sudden unsteady step, then bent into the car to retrieve her purse.

She's drunk.

She shut the car door and made the trek toward the front porch, still not seeing Tidwell.

She wore a dark, long-sleeve blouse that covered most of her bandages, and tight white skinny jeans. There was a bandage high on her forehead. She seemed to be talking to herself very quietly as she headed toward him.

When she got to the steps of the porch, she saw him and stopped cold.

"Greetings," he said.

"You scared me."

He shrugged. "Sorry." *Not sorry.*

Lady was so tired; she only glanced at Janet and laid her head back down.

"What are you doing?" She attempted a smile, but it came off as forced and fake.

His head craned back. "Me? I'm doing what I always do. What about you? You're the one who had the hot date."

"Pfft." Janet started up the steps and had to grab the rail to stop from falling.

"Where'd you go?" he said, angry she had been out drinking with another man, and that she had driven in that condition.

"A Mexican place. You don't know it." Her words were slurred.

"Margaritas I guess."

She stared at him coldly, swaying. "I suppose you haven't had anything to drink today."

"How many did you have?"

She scowled at him. "It's none of your business, Dolby. I'm sure it was much less than you've had."

In his mind, in his sober mind, he thought how sickening this was, how degrading, that they were both standing there drunk in the night, accusing each other with poisonous words meant to hurt and destroy. That they'd both driven while intoxicated.

He felt despicable.

He got to his feet, towering over her, as she was only halfway up the steps. "It is my business. You're my wife."

"Ha. Really? You could've fooled me."

"You need help getting up the steps?"

She cussed at him and climbed the rest of the steps with determination.

He got in her way at the top. "Why are you doing this?" he said. "I would never do this to you . . . see someone else."

She squinted at him and shook her head every which way. "Dolby, I've told you, you've changed—for the worse. And you're never sober enough to realize what's going on. I can't take it anymore. I'm not going to let you ruin my life."

"Oh." He bumped her slightly. "This is new. Now you can't take it anymore. So, it must've been a good date. I'm getting phased out . . . Does this guy know I'll kill him?"

The words slowly registered and changed Janet's expression to one of horror.

"What?" Tidwell said. "You think I'm gonna let this go on?"

"Get out of my way." She pushed him and went past.

"Do you want to know the latest on your son? I saw him today."

Janet got inside, gave him a nasty look, and slammed the door.

34

It was dark now as the two boys on their bikes made a sharp left on International Blvd., slanting so much that their plastic bags scraped the pavement. Clarence followed in the Malibu with Brandon at his side.

Brandon was in somewhat of a daze, coming to the realization that he may have to end the relationship with Kristen. It made him sick. What they'd initially had was gone. *Was it ever real in the first place?* It was as if she'd been acting in the beginning. He wondered if her interest in the Bible study was just her way of finding a guy. And he was the idiot who'd fallen for it. She needed help. He would try to guide her in the right direction, to get with a counselor, but he feared she wasn't going to let him break up that easily.

What a mess.

The two boys were now riding on the bumpy sidewalk. As the Malibu closed in on them, Clarence asked Brandon how he wanted to play it.

"Drive past them and park and we'll get out," Brandon said.

They passed the boys, who were not aware they were being watched.

"Further. Go down further," Brandon waved.

Clarence got about a hundred yards past the boys. "Here?"

"Yeah. Good."

Clarence pulled over, stopped the car, and started to get out.

"Hold up," Brandon said. "Wait till they get closer. You take the tall one, I'll take the short one. Just stop them."

Brandon and Clarence watched and waited.

The boys were forty feet away and approaching fast.

"Now," Brandon said.

He and Clarence got out in a flash and jogged toward the sidewalk.

Almost simultaneously, the boys' bikes screeched and skidded sideways as they hit the brakes with worry in their wide eyes.

"Hold on, hold on, we just want to talk," Brandon said, as he and Clarence grabbed the handlebars of both bikes.

"What is this?" the taller kid protested.

"It's that cop—from this morning," the smaller one said.

"That's right. My name's Brandon Deetz, Portland Police. We need to ask you some questions."

"You can't do this!" The boys both objected wildly, with outraged expressions, trying to yank their bikes away. The plastic bags attached to their handlebars overflowed with plastic bottles of window cleaner and rolls of paper towels.

"Cool down!" Clarence said. "Cool down. We aren't going to hurt you or keep you long. But you need to cooperate."

When the boys continued to argue, Clarence shook the one kid's bike and ordered him to be still. With that, the boys' mouths sealed shut, but they continued to fume, their foreheads both dripping with sweat.

"You said this morning you recognized the officer I was with—from a theater," Brandon said. "Were you referring to the night another officer was shot?"

"Don't say a word, Rodney," said the taller boy, out of breath. "You say anything and next thing you know you'll be in a courtroom testifying."

"Rodney," Brandon said, "that officer died that night. Were you there?"

"Shut your face, Rodney!" the taller boy ordered, shaking his head. "Don't you say a word."

"We need to know what happened that night," Brandon said. He pointed at Rodney. "You implied this morning that you saw that officer I was with at the theater that night—did you?"

"I'm telling you." The taller boy looked at Rodney threateningly.

"That cop should be in jail!" Rodney blurted.

The taller boy dropped his head.

"You should've heard what he said to us," Rodney said. "The cop that got shot defended us."

"You are so stupid, Rodney," the taller boy said. "You're gonna regret this."

"I don't care," Rodney said. "He was calling us names, the n-word, saying what lazy trash we was. Pushin' and shovin' us. All up in our business. The other cop said to stop."

Clarence and Brandon looked at each other.

"You were both there?" Brandon said.

After a moment, the boys nodded, barely.

"Then what?" Clarence said.

The boys stared at each other. Rodney piped up. "The cops argued. The good one yelled for the bad one to stop hating on us and the bad one called him an n-lover."

"He wasn't . . . the bad one wasn't gonna stop," the tall boy shook his head. "He was nuts. He was dissing us, dissing Blacks. He shoved Rodney, and another boy. He wanted to fight us. A cop!"

Rodney said, "A kid in the group had a thirty-eight. He yelled for the bad cop to stop."

"He wouldn't stop harassing us," the tall boy added.

"What's your name?" Brandon said to the tall boy.

"Leonard."

"So, what happened when your friend got his gun out?"

"The bad cop went for it," Rodney said.

"They wrestled," Leonard said. "The kid who had the gun bit him . . . bit the cop on his ear."

Clarence's and Brandon's eyes locked. Adrenaline sizzled between them like a live wire.

"What's your friend's name—who had the thirty-eight?"

"No way," Leonard said. He glared at Rodney and shook his head. "Not in a million years."

Brandon and Clarence looked at Rodney, the one who seemed to want to talk, but he followed Leonard's lead and shook his head no.

"What happened after the cop got bit?" Brandon said.

The boys were silent for a moment.

"They kept fighting for the gun and it went off," Leonard said, staring down at the sidewalk as if in a trance. "The other cop went down. It was bad."

Again, Brandon and Clarence stared at each other in disbelief.

"Blood was everywhere," Rodney said.

"The bad cop froze," Leonard said. "We all scattered."

"The boy with the gun?" Brandon said.

"He took off," Leonard said.

"With the gun?" Brandon said.

Both boys nodded.

"You've got to tell us his name," Clarence demanded.

Just then, Brandon noticed a huge red Chevy Silverado pickup truck with dark windows cruise past, and his stomach turned sour and instantly churned with terror.

Rickert drove a truck like that.

Clarence hadn't noticed.

"Look," Brandon said more urgently, "if you want to see that bad cop pay, you've got to give us the kid's name who had the gun."

The boys both squirmed. They appeared to want to talk, but they feared for their own safety.

Brandon was antsy. He kept watching for the red truck to come back.

Maybe it wasn't Rickert.

"He let the good cop die," Leonard broke the silence.

"What do you mean?" Clarence said.

"We watched. From behind the bushes," Leonard said.

"After you all took off?" Brandon said, his heart pounding.

The boys nodded.

"The bad cop waited to call for an ambulance because the good cop had seen what he done," Rodney said.

Brandon spotted the red truck coming down the street toward them. It had turned around! Brandon didn't want to say anything to Clarence for fear it would scare the boys.

"Wait, wait, wait," Clarence said, "you're saying the bad cop *let* the good cop die? Waited for him to die?"

"Yeah, 'cause he shot him. He knew he'd be in trouble if that cop lived."

Brandon felt as if the earth had shifted.

His face burned.

As the truck approached with its headlights on, Brandon tried to see through the windshield, because the side windows were too dark. A man was driving, holding a baseball cap up by his face as he glided past. It looked like Rickert. Brandon was chilled to the bone.

"Let us go!" Leonard said. "Please." He began trying to pull his bike away from Clarence, who was visibly shaken and furious.

"You want to let them go?" Clarence said.

"Where's the gun?" Brandon insisted.

The boys immediately looked at each other.

They knew.

"Does that kid still have it? Is it at his house?" Brandon said.

"It ain't at his house," Leonard said. "If we tell you where it is, will you let us go?"

"Yes, where is it?" Brandon said.

Leonard yanked his bike away from Clarence. "There's an abandoned house on Chariot with a 'no trespassing' sign; chain across the driveway." He reached over and pulled Rodney's bike away from Brandon. "In the woods behind it there's a well. It's down there."

35

THE PULSING sound of his cell phone in the pitch-black bedroom awoke Wayne Deetz with a start and instantly caused his heart to thunder. He'd set the phone to the sleep mode, only allowing calls from immediate family, so he knew it was either J.P. or Brandon. Joanie rolled over and mumbled, "Who is it?" as Deetz reached for the glowing phone on his nightstand.

The screen showed it was Brandon and he told her that.

"Hey, Son, what's up?"

"Hey, Dad, did I wake you?"

At least Brandon didn't sound hurt or in trouble.

"It's okay," Deetz said. "What's going on?"

"I didn't want to call Tidwell this late, but this can't wait." Brandon quickly explained all he and Clarence had learned in Conklin from Rodney and Leonard.

Joanie was propped up on one elbow, listening as Deetz asked questions.

After Brandon had told Deetz almost everything, he added the kicker about possibly seeing Harold Rickert drive past.

"What kind of car?" Deetz said.

"Big red Chevy Silverado," Brandon said.

"That's it, that's what he drives."

Deetz wanted to stand, to move, but the injured leg prevented him from doing so.

Joanie was out of bed now, putting on her robe.

"What should we do?" Brandon said. "We've got to get that gun."

Deetz was angry and frustrated that he couldn't go meet them himself. "I'll call Tidwell. Where are you guys?"

"We're heading toward that house on Chariot."

"Brandon, don't do anything till you hear from me, okay? We're going to need help getting into that well. It may have to wait till tomorrow—"

"What about Rickert?"

"Let me talk to Tidwell. Okay? I'll get right back to you."

The instant they hung up, Joanie said, "I hope you don't think you're going anywhere."

"Just hold on," Deetz said, "I've got to call Tidwell. I may have him pick me up."

Deetz knew that would bring a barrage of objections from Joanie, which it did. But he quickly explained to her what was going on as he dialed Tidwell.

"I don't care if the precinct is on fire—you're not going anywhere!"

Deetz held up an index finger urging her to wait, just wait.

Tidwell picked up on the second ring.

Joanie left the room fuming and headed toward the kitchen.

Tidwell sounded as if he'd been drinking.

Deetz relayed everything Brandon had told him.

"I better go out there now," Tidwell said. "I don't want Rickert beating us to it. I'll have fire and rescue meet us out there. I'll call Brandon and tell him I'm coming."

Deetz made sure Joanie wasn't within earshot. "I'm on your way," he said quietly. "You want to pick me up?"

There was a distinct pause.

"Wayne, no, you don't have to go out there. It'll just slow me down. And Joanie would have my hide."

"Come on, man—"

"No, Wayne. I've got Brandon and Clarence out there. You need to go back to bed and rest. Get better. You'll be back soon enough."

"Dolby, are you okay?"

Silence.

"Dolby?"

"I'm fine, Wayne. Why?"

"To be honest, you sound like you've been drinking."

"Ah, just a beer or two. Don't worry. I'm cool. You get better now."

They ended the call and Deetz was flustered. How was he supposed to sleep now?

"Hey," Joanie whispered as she walked back into the bedroom with her arms crossed. "You need anything?"

"I'm wide awake now."

"Well, I see you came to your senses."

"No, actually, Tidwell didn't want to pick me up. He said you'd kill him and I'd slow him down."

"Amazing. You want some hot tea or water? Something to eat?"

"No, thanks."

She took her robe off and started getting back into bed. "I'm going to read for a bit."

"I will too, I guess."

He looked at his phone one last time and opened the Find My Friends app. The map showed that Brandon was indeed approaching Chariot Street. He turned the phone off and silently prayed for God's protection—and that they would find what they were looking for.

36

PART of the reason Tidwell didn't want to pick up Deetz was because he had quite a buzz on. He didn't want Deetz smelling the alcohol on his breath, evaluating his driving, or getting up in his business.

Tidwell strapped on his holster, checked the magazine from his Glock, holstered the weapon, and threw a coat on over it. He went down the hallway, listened at Janet's door for a moment, heard nothing, then knocked quietly.

"Yes," she said.

He opened the door. The lights were out. She was lying on her back in bed holding her glowing cellphone in front of her face.

As he stepped into the black room, Tidwell wondered if she was communicating with Greg Stovall but bit his lip.

"I've got to go over to Conklin," he said. "We may've found the gun that killed Lance. It's supposedly at the bottom of a well."

This was big news. Janet loved Lance like a brother. Tidwell thought it might bring them closer together.

"Are you really in any condition to do that?" she said.

"I'm fine."

She shrugged and looked back her phone. "Be careful."

That was her cold way of saying, "Here you go again, the drunk workaholic off to feed his habits."

He said nothing and just stared at her as she scrolled through her phone.

His teeth clenched as he shut the door with a slight bang.

He stood there in the hallway getting madder by the second at the thought of her video chatting or texting with another man.

He headed for the fridge, grabbed two bottles of beer, patted Lady, and took off for his car.

FIVE MINUTES and one beer into the twenty-minute drive, Tidwell had thought it all through and was about to call fire and rescue, then Brandon Deetz, when his phone rang.

He didn't recognize the number but accepted the call over speaker. "Yeah."

There was a pause.

He heard heavy breathing coming from the other end of the line.

"Sergeant Tidwell. Harold Rickert."

Tidwell's heart stopped for a second and the wheels in his head spun.

What could he want?

"Yes, Rickert. What can I do for you?" Tidwell had to pretend he didn't know anything about Rickert's foul play the night Lance died.

"Call off your men at the house on Chariot. Right now."

Tidwell wondered how Rickert found out and began to protest.

"Or else," Rickert cut him off, "I'll arrest your son for dealing crystal meth. I know he's working with the Grimaldi crew. I know he and his partner are dealing out of their ambulance. I know he's in debt for thousands of dollars. I know he's using like a junkie. Call off the men at the house on Chariot and I keep my mouth shut."

Tidwell's knee-jerk reaction was to drink. He took a swig of beer and considered how to answer. His heart was ticking like a time bomb and his rage was mounting.

"You killed Lance Burke," he said quietly, evenly.

"Call off those men—"

"You were harassing those boys! One had a gun and you went for it. He bit you!"

"You know how much time your son will get? At least twenty years, probably more."

Tidwell couldn't stand the thought of it.

He was drunk.

He was a miserable mess.

Now, here he was in the middle of a blackmail scandal.

But if he could keep Nick from going to jail, he had to do it.

He thought through the steps. If he told Brandon and Clarence to go home. If he never called fire and rescue. If—

"Call off those men and meet me there. I've got rope," Rickert said. "We'll get the evidence. My problem will be solved and so will your son's."

"Brandon Deetz and Clarence Waters know, you idiot. They know what you did! I'm not the only one."

"Nothing is going to happen to me unless a gun is produced. You help me get that gun and your son remains a free man."

Rickert was right. If Tidwell and he could find the gun and make it disappear, the lack of evidence would make the case against Rickert go away, no matter what anyone said.

"How did you find out about the gun?" Tidwell said.

"Never mind that. Are you going to work with me or not? Because I swear, if you say no, I'm picking up your son right now— tonight. He and his buddy just got a new batch of product. That's why they were at that house your boy was running from. Me and Brandon Deetz interrupted the handoff. But they have it now and it's on them in the ambo. So, what's it going to be, Sarge? We haven't got all night."

Tidwell was distraught.

He used to be a good man. Honest. Trustworthy. A man of authority.

Now he was weak. Filth. Janet was right about him. He couldn't blame her for anything she was doing.

Where are you? He wondered silently to God.

If Tidwell did this deal with Rickert there would be no turning back. He would be guilty not only of covering up Nick's drug dealing, but also covering up Lance's murder.

He envisioned Nick in orange prison coveralls with an inmate number stenciled on back, getting pummeled by a gang of thugs. He would never last in there.

Maybe it's what he needs.

"Make a decision!" Rickert broke the silence.

"Yes. Okay . . . I'll do it."

As soon as the words left his mouth, Tidwell felt as if he'd bitten a poisoned apple.

"Yes, you'll do what?" Rickert said.

"Call them off. Meet you there."

"Twenty minutes," Rickert said.

Tidwell looked at the time and determined he may need more than that depending on how it went down with Brandon and Clarence. "I'll text you when it's clear. It'll be twenty to thirty minutes."

"Fine. Make it fast."

37

IT WAS AFTER 10 P.M. Brandon and Clarence sat in the Malibu with the windows down, parked at the curb in front of the abandoned house on Chariot Street. The night had turned chilly but was pleasant. The neighborhood was dark and relatively quiet. Now and then a bicycle or two went by in the street ridden by hyped-up kids. Several groups of people could be heard but not seen nearby. Brandon smelled cigarette smoke in the air, possibly floating over from some of the neighbors who huddled on sagging front porches.

Brandon had received a text from his dad ten minutes earlier stating that Tidwell would be on his way, along with local fire and rescue in an attempt to retrieve the gun from the well.

Although it was quite dark, Brandon could see that the short driveway of the home was cracked and drastically uneven. A rusted chain drooped across the driveway with a red and white 'no trespassing' sign hanging from it, almost touching the ground.

The house itself was a dump. It looked haunted. The roof was caving in, several windows were broken, the railing along the front porch was rotted black, and the steps leading up to the house were slanted, one with a gaping hole in it.

The front yard was small, just like all the other houses along Chariot. An enormous tree in the front yard prevented much grass from growing beneath it and its massive roots protruded like knots throughout the front yard, which was mostly dirt.

"How am I supposed to ride with Rickert tomorrow, knowing all this is going down?" Clarence said.

"If we find the gun tonight you may not have to worry about it," Brandon said.

"You think they'd arrest him that fast?"

"I do. It'll be up to Tidwell—"

Brandon's phone vibrated. He checked the screen.

"That's him now," Brandon said, then answered the call.

"Brandon, your dad filled me in on everything," Tidwell said. "Good work to track down those boys."

"Thank you. Yeah, Clarence and I are here in front of the house on Chariot. Fire and rescue haven't arrived yet."

"Is anyone else there?"

"No, sir, just us."

"Okay, great job. Listen . . . I need you guys to call it a night—"

Brandon's heart stopped.

Tidwell continued. "You've put in a full day, a really good day. I'll meet fire and rescue and we'll take it from there."

What?

Tidwell's words hit Brandon like snow in summer—all wrong. He glanced at Clarence with a look of bewilderment.

"Sir, we really want to see this through," Brandon said. "We're here. Can't we just wait for you? We're off the clock."

Tidwell was silent for a moment. "I appreciate your commitment, Brandon. Tell Clarence thank you as well. But there's no need for you guys to hang around. If the property is what I'm envisioning, it will be a liability for us to have you out there, especially when you're not on duty."

Brandon was in shock. "I don't know what to say, Sergeant. This just seems . . . weird to me."

Silence again.

Then Tidwell's voice took on a hint of coldness. "Just trust me on this one. Your night is over. Great job. I'll let you guys know what we find. Good night."

Click.

Brandon stared at the phone.

"What was that all about?" Clarence said.

"He's sending us home." Brandon repeated what Tidwell had said.

They both sat there, stunned, not wanting to leave.

Brandon had the urge to call his dad and vent to him.

"Don't mark my words on this," Brandon said, "but he sounded like he'd been drinking."

"Oh man, that's weird you say that," Clarence said. "The other night when his wife got in that wreck, I honestly thought I smelled booze on him. He kept backing away from me."

"Something's not right. Maybe I should call my dad."

Clarence looked all around. "I wonder if we can park somewhere and watch what happens."

Brandon looked around, too. "Rickert will recognize your car."

"And if Tidwell sees us we'll be in trouble."

Brandon made a decision. "I'm calling my dad." He started dialing Deetz on his phone.

"What do you want me to do?" Clarence said. "Should we stay here?"

"We better cruise. Just get away from here for a few minutes."

After about four rings Deetz finally picked up his phone. "What is it now, Son?"

"Clarence and I are at the house on Chariot and Tidwell called and told us to go home."

The line was silent.

Clarence started the car and eased away from the curb.

"Dad?"

"Yeah, I'm thinking," Deetz said.

"Why would he do that?" Brandon pleaded. "He sounded like he'd been drinking, FYI."

"I'm confused," Deetz said. "Tidwell told me he was going to meet you out there, with fire and rescue. Did he say why he wants you to leave?"

"We put in a long day . . . we're not on the clock so we'd be a liability on that private property—"

"Are you still there?"

"We're just driving around now. We're going to stay close."

Clarence made a turn onto the next street over and drove very slowly.

"Was anyone else there yet?" Deetz said.

"No."

"Okay, look, you better just do what he says," Deetz said. "He has his reasons. Just call it a night. He'll let us know. I'm confused, too, Brandon, but he's the boss."

"Somethings wrong, Dad."

Deetz was silent, as if trying to figure out what was going on.

Brandon heard his mom in the background, asking Deetz what was going on.

Clarence made another right and his headlights swept over two wrecked bicycles . . . and the two boys they'd talked with earlier, now both crumpled on the sidewalk, leaning against a tree, as if they were recovering from a beating.

38

TIDWELL FELT AWFUL.

Dirty.

The weight of the world on him.

As he came within two minutes of getting to the house on Chariot, and the supposed well, he was plagued with guilt. He was about to partner with the man who killed Lance Burke.

For what?

For his son's freedom.

Tidwell finished off the second beer.

What am I doing?

Tidwell realized if he was caught in this scheme, it would not only be the end of his career, but likely prison.

But what were his options? If he got the gun and arrested Rickert, Rickert would blow the whistle on Nick. And Rickert had been right, Nick's life would be ruined. He'd be behind bars until he was forty or fifty.

Tidwell couldn't fathom that.

He couldn't let it happen.

Brandon Deetz had been upset that Tidwell had sent Clarence and him home. As Tidwell turned onto Chariot, he told himself he would need to check the area thoroughly to make sure they had really left the scene.

He drove slowly, casing the area.

The street was quite dark with only a streetlight here and there.

He passed three boys walking, and down a bit further, on a corner, several men talking.

A cigarette glowed from a dark front porch. He smelled the smoke.

He came upon the abandoned house, chain across the driveway. He parked at the curb and turned the car off.

No sign of Brandon and Clarence.

He texted Rickert:

I'm here. Alone.

Tidwell looked all around, wondering how the heck they were going to find a well in the black woods behind the house. He reached over and got his black metal flashlight out of the glove compartment. He felt for his gun, under his coat, just to make sure he was armed up.

Lights from behind flooded his car.

Rickert in his big truck, with its massive grill, came to a stop right behind Tidwell. *He must've just been cruising the area.* Rickert's lights went out and he jumped out of the truck.

Tidwell got out.

Rickert approached with a huge coil of rope over one shoulder and his holstered gun over the other. "Let's do this," he said.

Rickert wore black cargo pants and a plain, dark T-shirt. He climbed over the chain and headed along the right side of the house, carrying a big flashlight that he hadn't turned on yet.

Tidwell followed, keeping his light out as well. He looked back to the street to make sure Brandon and Clarence hadn't followed. Or anyone else.

Rickert's flashlight went on when he got to the woods and he went right in as if he'd done it a hundred times before. The guy was hard core for sure.

Tidwell turned on his flashlight and followed.

The ground was damp and the leaves on the brush were wet.

They were twenty feet in when Rickert stopped and turned around to face Tidwell. "Don't follow me. Branch off or we'll never find it."

Tidwell's face flushed. He was infuriated. But the jerk was right. So, Tidwell fanned off to the left and waded his way forward, through the wet trees, realizing he was tipsy, and wondering what in God's name he'd gotten himself into.

The longer they looked, the more Tidwell began to wonder what would happen if they didn't find it at all. Maybe it wasn't real. Maybe this whole thing was a story.

If they didn't find the gun, there would be no evidence against Rickert in Lance's death. Only the word of those boys.

And Rickert would still own Tidwell because he knew about Nick's involvement with Grimaldi's drug crew.

Tidwell smacked a mosquito on the back of his neck and cussed, incensed by the despicable hole he had dug for himself. Walking through the wet woods in the night, acting like a criminal while his wife cheated on him and his son sold death drugs from an ambulance!

And that girl, Deborah. It was Tidwell's fault she was in the morgue.

Tidwell continued trudging through the woods, his steps feeling like a moon walk.

You're drunk.

You're a sergeant with the Portland Police Bureau—and you're drunk, in the woods, doing a very bad thing.

"Got it," Rickert called through the trees. "Over here."

Tidwell saw Rickert's flashlight shake back and forth through the trees and brush.

"Coming," Tidwell called, and ambled off toward the light.

39

"YOU BETTER CALL YOUR OLD MAN," Clarence said out of breath as he and Brandon got back into Clarence's car after learning what had happened to the two boys, Rodney and Leonard.

"Dude, he's trying to recover. I've already woken him up once," Brandon said. "Besides, there's nothing he can do. We need to go back to that house; this thing is going down."

"Tidwell told us to stand down, man." Clarence said as he started the Malibu and eased out onto the street.

"That was *before* Rickert did what he did to those boys. Tidwell might be in trouble. Rickert's going for that gun."

"Man, I don't like this," Clarence said as he drove toward the abandoned house on Chariot.

"We've got to at least cruise by," Brandon said. "Let's just see what's up."

Clarence drove in silence, murmuring about how they shouldn't be going against Tidwell's orders.

But Rickert had roughed up Rodney and Leonard until they'd told him everything they'd told Brandon and Clarence—which meant Rickert now knew about the gun in the well. Brandon was sure the man would do everything in his power to find that evidence as quickly as possible—as was evidenced by the red marks, bruises, and torn clothes left on Rodney and Leonard.

"We have their names and addresses now," Clarence said.

"They're witnesses. Maybe we should just call it a night—like the Sergeant ordered."

"Bro, witnesses—kid witnesses—aren't going to matter one bit if there's no evidence. Besides, he's got them scared so bad they may not speak up anyway. You saw that. They were totally freaked out."

The boys said Rickert told them that if they ever testified against him, he would sneak into their homes, kidnap them, and no one would ever see them again.

Clarence turned slowly onto Chariot.

"Hurry up, dude," Brandon said.

"For the record, I don't think we should be doing this."

They approached the abandoned house.

"No fire and rescue," Brandon said. "And that's Rickert's truck."

"And Tidwell's Charger," Clarence said.

"Why no fire and rescue?" Brandon said. "Tidwell said he was calling them."

Clarence cruised past the house and past Tidwell's Charger and Rickert's pickup. Then he kept going.

"Hold up, we need to go back," Brandon said.

"No way."

"Dude, stop. Tidwell may be in trouble. He didn't know Rickert knew about the well."

Clarence pulled over to the curb, put it in park, leaned over the steering wheel, and glared at Brandon. "Remember what Tidwell said about us being off duty . . . being a liability? We could get sued if something goes wrong."

"Go back, Clarence. Tidwell may have been going to get the gun alone. I'm telling you, he didn't know Rickert was going to show up."

"Did you ever think they may be working together?" Clarence said.

The words seemed to slap Brandon across the face.

He sat there staring at Clarence, putting two and two together.

"Tidwell wouldn't do that," Brandon said hesitantly, with doubt in his voice. "Lance was his best friend . . ."

"Maybe Rickert's blackmailing Tidwell," Clarence said. "You

know, 'I'll keep my mouth shut about Nick if you help me make the gun disappear.'"

Brandon shook his head, not wanting that to be true.

"Look man, just go back," Brandon said. "You can stay in the car if you want. Or drop me off. I don't care."

Clarence looked at him long and hard.

Then, suddenly, he wheeled the Malibu around and headed back toward the abandoned house, mumbling about what trouble they were getting themselves into.

40

By the time Tidwell made his way through the thick brush to the well, Rickert had already tied his rope to a nearby tree. As Tidwell approached, Rickert tossed the rope down into the dark abyss and stared up at Tidwell.

The well's opening was about four feet in circumference, circled by a small, ancient stone wall about three feet high. The stones were dark with moss and several had crumbled and a few had fallen away.

"I'd send you down, but I don't think you'd make it back up," Rickert said as he kneeled, leaned over the edge, and shined his light down toward the bottom of the well. Tidwell wondered whether Rickert had said that because Tidwell was so big and somewhat out of shape—or because Rickert realized he had been drinking.

"There's no water at the bottom, is there?" Tidwell said, looking down into the black vertical tunnel.

"What do you think, genius?"

Tidwell's face burned. The fact that Rickert felt he could talk down to Tidwell made Tidwell realize Rickert believed he had the sergeant right where he wanted him.

"It's got to be dry," Rickert said, pulling hard at the rope tied to the tree, to make sure it was secure.

"You think you have enough rope?" Tidwell shown his light into the well, but all he could see was the rope leading into darkness.

"I'll find out when I get down there." Rickert stepped toward Tidwell, and glared at him, his big eyes reflecting the light from the flashlights. "Listen to me, Sarge. If you try anything, you *and* your son are finished. That's a promise."

Tidwell nodded, his heart rate kicking up a notch, wondering if Rickert's cellphone would work from down in the well. Wondering if he should untie the rope once Rickert got down there, once he'd found the gun; he'd be caught red-handed.

But if Tidwell arrested Rickert, he would call out Nick, and that would be the end of him. His boy would go to prison for a long, long time.

Tidwell looked all around, unable to see the house or street from where they were. He knew better than most people that crooked schemes like this almost never succeeded. What was he thinking, going in on this coverup with Rickert of all people?

Without another word, Rickert put a leg over the edge of the short wall, tugged at the rope, made sure his holster was secure, and started down into the darkness.

If they could get this over with quickly and successfully, Tidwell would seek out LaRocca or Grimaldi tomorrow and try to pay off Nick's debt; get him out of that mess.

He shook his head and looked all around again. *You of all people should know this isn't going to work.*

Tidwell was so tense; he felt helpless. Defeated. Beaten.

The vibration of Tidwell's phone startled him. He quickly worked it out of his pocket. The glowing screen showed a text from Brandon Deetz:

> Sarge, Rickert beat those two boys tonight after we talked to them. They told him the gun is in the well. Are you ok? We are here. Rickert's car is here. Do you need help?

Tidwell cussed and shook the phone.

Clenching his teeth in desperation, he leaned over the short wall and shined his flashlight down on Rickert, who was repelling like an expert rock climber. Rickert noticed the light and shot a glance up toward Tidwell, but ignored it and continued dropping down, down.

Tidwell was beside himself knowing Brandon and Clarence were within a hundred yards of him and probably suspicious of his dirty deed.

He didn't know what to do. He couldn't recall a time when he'd been so indecisive.

Think. Think!

He examined his phone, re-read the text from Brandon, and hurriedly typed out a response:

I ordered you guys to go home.

Send.

Almost immediately a response came back from Brandon:

Where's fire and rescue?

Tidwell swore and shook and blew a gasket. Feeling the sweat on his forehead, he pounded out a response:

I'm handling this. They'll be here. You guys go.
That's an order. I'm fine.

Send.

They may not leave. Brandon was exactly like his father—a justice seeker. Good police to the core. Which was exactly what Tidwell *did not* need right now.

Tidwell was sick with guilt and fear and paranoia.

The rope moved suddenly. Tidwell touched it. It was slack! Rickert must have hit the ground.

Tidwell shined his light into the well and could see only the rope dangling into blackness.

He paced.

Panic coursed through his veins.

His heart thundered.

He could rip that rope up right this second and Rickert would be stuck, trapped.

But, to what end?

It would give Tidwell time.

Time to get to LaRocca, pay Nick's debt.

But then what?

No, no, no. That makes no sense.

Tidwell leaned back over the wall, shined his light down again, and called out: "Did you find it?"

There was no answer.

Tidwell put his ear to the opening. He could hear the faint sound of Rickert groping around, searching.

Tidwell walked away from the well, perhaps ten yards, and got out his phone. He turned it on and scrolled until he found what he was looking for: "I will lead the blind by ways they have not known. Along unfamiliar paths I will guide them. I will turn the darkness into light before them. And make the rough places smooth. These are the things I will do; I will not forsake them."

Tidwell turned off the phone. He embraced the darkness, wanted to disappear with it.

You are better than this.

Rickert had done the unthinkable, letting Lance die, waiting until he bled out!

But . . . Nick.

Prison.

Tidwell's phone vibrated. It was a call. He got it out. The bright screen told him it was Wayne Deetz.

Tidwell headed back toward the well, put the phone to his ear, and spoke very quietly. "Tidwell."

"Dolby, it's Wayne."

"What's up?"

"I haven't been able to sleep. Did you find the gun?"

Tidwell thought, *if only he knew what was happening.* "Not yet. We're looking." *Looking . . . with Harold Rickert.*

"Okay, listen, I've got an idea," Deetz said. "What if you were to have Nick turn state's evidence against Grimaldi, D-Love, the whole operation. He'll get leniency for bringing down such a big fish. He could even get immunity."

Tidwell stood there—shellshocked.

It was bad and it was good.

He hadn't thought of it.

His heart raced.

He got his flashlight from his belt and directed the bright beam into the well.

Rickert was in view, climbing back up.

"Dolby, are you there?"

"Yeah," Tidwell whispered.

"I know it would be hard, but look, the way Nick's going—"

"I get you."

"He's going to get arrested sooner or later, and if that happens, they'll throw the book at him. But if he turns himself in with evidence against—"

"I heard you, Wayne," Tidwell said sharply, immediately sorry. "Thanks. I've got to go."

41

BRANDON LED the way with his flashlight through the damp brush behind the abandoned house on Chariot, and Clarence was just a few feet behind him with his own light.

"Dude, this is not cool," Clarence whispered. "Tidwell gave us a direct order to go home. I'm not feelin' this at all."

"Shhh." Brandon forged ahead, zigzagging to avoid limbs and thick brush. "Tidwell may be in trouble."

"Yeah, *we* may be in trouble . . . with Rickert out here? This has 'disaster' written all over it."

"Turn your light off," Brandon said. "Mine's enough. Just stay close to me."

Clarence did so and they continued deeper into the woods, walking as quietly as possible, watching, and listening for anything.

"Dang it," Clarence hissed. "These mosquitoes are eating me alive. Come on, man, let's go back. I honestly do not have a good feeling about this."

"Go back if you want, Clarence. I've got to do this—"

Brandon heard something. "Shhh!" He turned his light out and stopped suddenly, throwing a hand up for Clarence to stop and be silent.

Brandon pointed through the trees toward the beam of a flashlight about forty feet in front of them.

"Did you find it?" That was Tidwell's voice, calling down into the well.

Brandon and Clarence were silent.

Brandon's heart pounded.

Could Rickert be down in the well?

Tidwell suddenly pulled away from the opening of the well and walked directly toward Brandon and Clarence.

Brandon could barely breathe.

Tidwell examined the glowing screen of his phone for a few moments, then put it away.

Brandon and Clarence stood as still and silent as possible.

There was a faint hum. Tidwell got his phone out again. It lit up. He turned and walked back toward the well and answered a call.

Brandon couldn't make out the few words Tidwell spoke. It seemed he was mainly listening.

Tidwell leaned over the well and shined his light down in while he was still on the phone.

Brandon waved at Clarence to follow him, and he inched forward, closer to the well.

∾

TIDWELL PUT the phone in his pocket and suddenly felt certain to the core that the call from Wayne Deetz was God leading him along the unfamiliar path, turning the darkness into light.

A flicker of hope arose deep inside him. He quickly went over several ways this could play out in his mind, while Rickert grunted and made his way back up to the surface of the well.

Tidwell's adrenaline pounded through his veins. "Find it?"

Rickert said nothing. Sweat covered his face. He looked up and reached out a hand toward Tidwell.

There was a pause. In that split-second, Tidwell's eyes locked with Rickert's. They both knew this could go a hundred different ways.

Tidwell extended his big hand and pulled Rickert up over the edge.

Rickert went to the ground and caught his breath.

"Well?" Tidwell said.

"I got it." Rickert got to his knees, then quickly to his feet. He untied the rope from the tree and wrapped it around his hand and elbow repeatedly, coiling it as they stood there.

"Let's see it," Tidwell said, feeling this thing was about to explode.

"No need for that," Rickert said. "Let's get out of here."

"Hold it." Tidwell ordered. "I want to see it."

"Why? You don't believe me?" Rickert chuckled, reached behind his back, and patted the waistband of his pants. "It's here safe and sound. Now let's go."

Rickert turned from Tidwell, flicked on his flashlight, and began walking back toward the house.

That's it.

Tidwell quietly drew his Glock from its holster and racked the slide. Rickert stopped but did not turn around.

Tidwell trained the gun on Rickert's back.

"Put your hands on your head; clasp them." Tidwell's heart raced as he approached Rickert. "Get on your knees."

Rickert only stood there, rock solid with his hands at his sides. "Are you arresting me?"

Tidwell feared Rickert may spin on him and go for his gun; and, knowing Rickert, he wouldn't have to rack his—he would already have a bullet in the chamber.

"If you're arresting me," Rickert said, "you better make sure you have the evidence. Do I have it, or not?" He laughed.

"Hands on your head and drop to your knees!" Tidwell commanded.

Rickert did not move a muscle. "You're not going to shoot me, Sarge. Especially in the back."

Before Tidwell could say another word, Rickert slowly turned on his flashlight—and began walking away very slowly.

"Stop Rickert!" Tidwell had to trust Deetz, he had to trust God —that Nick would be okay. "I'm arresting you for the murder of Lance Burke, my best friend. Now stop!"

It was dark, but Tidwell zeroed in his aim on Rickert's upper body as best he could, wondering if the man was so miserable that he wanted to die, praying the man would stop so he didn't have to shoot him.

～

BRANDON AND CLARENCE watched breathlessly from twenty-five feet away in the shadow of the trees and brush.

When Rickert ignored Tidwell's order for the second time, Brandon quietly removed his gun from its holster. He nodded at Clarence, who did the same.

"Stay here," Brandon whispered and pointed to the right, "I'm going around that way."

Clarence nodded.

Brandon got perhaps twelve feet away from Clarence when he heard Tidwell yell, "Stop Rickert! I'm arresting you for . . ."

Brandon stopped, quietly racked his gun, trained it on Rickert as best he could through the woods, and watched with bated breath.

Rickert stood there with his flashlight on for another moment, then suddenly dove and rolled in a blur.

A gunshot flashed and rang out from Tidwell's Glock.

He'd missed.

The bouncing beam of Rickert's flashlight lit up the trees to Brandon's right.

Tidwell followed Rickert with this flashlight, but Brandon was going to be closer.

The beam of Rickert's flashlight bobbed and jiggled and got closer.

Brandon's heart hammered. He could hear Rickert grunting and dodging trees and obstacles. He was close.

Brandon forced himself to breathe. Ordered himself to go on the attack. But suddenly, he was bathed in light. Brandon looked down at his stomach and legs—to make sure it was true and, yes, his body was lit up like a billboard.

Brandon looked up, directly into Rickert's blinding flashlight, which was now stopped. Brandon saw a glint of light reflect off Rickert's gun, which was pointed directly at Brandon's chest, and he thought to himself, *You're dead.*

BAM. BAM.

The explosions of sound and light and ferocity came from Brandon's left.

His first thought was, *I'm hit.*

But he was still standing.

He felt no pain.

He smelled gunpowder.

His ears rang.

Rickert's flashlight dropped to the ground.

His body crumpled over it.

Clarence stepped in and put his big arm around Brandon.

Tidwell appeared out of breath, the beam of his flashlight hitting a wide-eyed Clarence, then Brandon, then the writhing body of Harold Rickert.

EPILOGUE

It was a pleasant summer afternoon some four weeks later, and they were all there—at Tidwell's house in Cedar Mill on the west side of Portland. There was a breeze in the air, the grill was smoking hot, the smell of charcoal and sweet corn and fresh cut grass filled the Tidwell's large front lawn as evening approached.

Lady sat right out in the middle of the circle of lawn chairs, with Leena lying next to her, petting her to death and swatting at the gnats. They were surrounded by Wayne and Joanie Deetz, Brandon and Kristen, J.P. and Tammy. Clarence was there, too, along with police colleagues Angie Cook and Sid Sikorski.

Nick adjusted the smooth jazz on the Bluetooth speaker and quietly went over to check on his dad at the grill. Meanwhile, Janet hurried about refilling beverages and replenishing appetizers.

Deetz sat there feeling just about as thankful as he'd ever been. He'd gone back to work two weeks ago and had ditched the crutches three days ago. He had a whole new appreciation for just being able to get around normally. He quickly did the math in his head and realized he had just a little over four months remaining before his big retirement at the end of the year. He would miss working with Tidwell and Angie and Sid, and many others on the force, but he would be ready to hang it up.

Kristen was in a deep conversation with Tammy, who'd become somewhat of a mentor to her over the past month. At Brandon's request, Tammy had referred Kristen to a counselor, whom she'd been seeing twice a week. Kristen had also been going to a women's group that Tammy had attended for several years. Brandon seemed content with Kristen's state of mind and when Deetz asked him earlier that day what the future looked like, Brandon had simply said he planned to, "Play it fast and loose and see how it all shakes out." Deetz and Joanie had their doubts, but they too had agreed they would keep it positive and see what developed.

Meanwhile, Leena was devouring cheese and crackers as if they were set out only for her. "Leena," Deetz whispered, "don't eat too many of those . . . save room for dinner." With a mouthful, she gave him an exaggerated roll of the eyes.

Deetz watched with a great feeling of satisfaction as Tidwell flipped burgers and turned hotdogs. Tidwell and son Nick had been attending morning AA meetings at the church where Tidwell originally visited. The first time they went together, they each picked up a round white plastic AA chip designating the start of their commitment to sobriety. In the AA system, different colored chips were used to celebrate successful recovery milestones.

Funny enough, the little guy Tidwell had run off the road, Neil Houser, had since become Tidwell's AA sponsor and close friend. Nick had also signed up with an AA sponsor more his age and appeared clean and sober. He was a shy young man, and it was obvious to Deetz he was finding things to do around the grill and in the house so he didn't have to sit and talk with anyone. He'd gained weight while his dad had lost about fifteen pounds; they both looked healthy.

After the night Rickert was shot, Nick had convinced his friend and EMT partner, Marty Martin, to join him in attempting to turn state's evidence against Sidney Grimaldi, Antonio D. LaRocca, and several additional higher ups who worked for Grimaldi.

To that end, Nick and Marty were currently working undercover with Portland police and prosecutors to gather names, dates, times, photos, and videos of Grimaldi's drug operation. Deetz was working behind the scenes with them. Attorneys said if Nick and Marty were successful in helping the prosecution put Grimaldi and company behind bars—potentially for life—they would likely receive immunity agreements as well as participation in the U.S.

Federal Witness Security Program for protection from Grimaldi and company.

Harold Rickert did not die the night Clarence shot him in the woods behind the abandoned house on Chariot Street. At the bottom of the well that night, he had indeed found the .38 special that had killed officer Lance Burke. Rickert recovered, was officially charged with Lance's murder, and was in custody at the Columbia River Correctional Institution awaiting trial.

In addition to the two teen witnesses, Leonard and Rodney, four additional boys had been found or come forward and would serve as witnesses against Rickert at his trial, including the boy who had originally produced the .38 special, wrestled with Rickert, and bit his ear. The boy's name was Wesley Brack, well-spoken, and anxious to testify.

The story of Lance's death and the new sinister twist involving Rickert had dominated Portland's news outlets since it had surfaced.

Rickert, meanwhile, had not only maintained his innocence, but had secured legal counsel to file a civil suit in Portland state court against Tidwell and the Portland Police Bureau for slander, libel, and defamation of character. He was seeking monetary damages for pain and suffering, for damage to his reputation, for lost wages, and for personal emotional suffering including shame and humiliation.

As the sun slowly went down and Deetz watched everyone at the picnic, picking up on bits and pieces of various conversations, he turned to see Janet approach Dolby at the grill. She tugged at his apron, looked up at him, and said something quietly with a smile; he, in turn, tilted his head back and laughed heartily. They had finally met with their marriage counselor for the first time and were impressed and hopeful.

"Okay everybody, burgers and dogs are ready," Tidwell said. "Grab a plate and buns and let me know what you want."

Tidwell had been sober ever since the night Rickert got shot. He'd also taken three weeks' vacation from work to devote to Janet, Nick, and Lady. Janet had given up the relationship with Greg Stovall as soon as she saw that Tidwell meant business about getting his life—their lives—back on track. Tidwell and Janet even showed up at Deetz's church, and Tidwell later told Deetz he was considering getting baptized.

Things were indeed looking up.

Everyone stood. People talked and meandered. No one rushed to get plates—besides Leena.

Tidwell held up a hand. "I'm going to ask Wayne to bless the food for us."

It got quiet. Everyone got still.

"Uh, let me say something first," Janet said. "We're very glad you could all make it. We're so grateful for your friendship—and support. Real quickly, I just wanted to give a shout out to my boys, Dolby and Nick, because just recently—I'm going to embarrass you —they got some new chips, and I'm not talking about potato chips."

Tidwell and Nick looked at each other. Nick's face turned red, he shook his head, and Tidwell smiled and dug into his pocket, nodding for Nick to do the same.

"They just got . . . new *red* chips for thirty days of sobriety."

The two men held up their red plastic AA chips, locked eyes with each other, nodded as if they had a secret pact, and received a raucous round of applause.

WHAT'S NEXT FROM CRESTON?

Creston is working on Book #7 in the Signs of Life Series!

Until then, check out his very latest stand-alone thriller,
CELEBRITY PASTOR, available on Amazon.

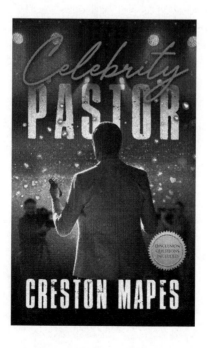

Creston Mapes grew up in northeast Ohio, where he has fond memories of living with his family of five in the upstairs portion of his dad's early American furniture store - The Weathervane Shop. Creston was not a good student, but the one natural talent he possessed was writing.

He set type by hand and cranked out his own neighborhood newspaper as a kid, then went on to graduate with a degree in journalism from Bowling Green State University. Creston was a newspaper reporter and photographer in Ohio and Florida, then moved to Atlanta, Georgia, for a job as a creative copywriter.

Creston served for a stint as a creative director, but quickly learned he was not cut out for management. He went out on his own as a freelance writer in 1991 and, over the next 30 years, did work for Chick-fil-A, Coca-Cola, The Weather Channel, Oracle, ABC-TV, TNT Sports, colleges and universities, ad agencies, and more. He's ghost-written more than ten non-fiction books.

Creston has penned many contemporary thrillers, achieved Amazon Bestseller status multiple times, and had one of his novels (*Nobody*) optioned as a major motion picture.

Creston married his fourth-grade sweetheart, Patty, and they have four amazing adult children. Creston loves his part-time job as an usher at local venues where he gets to see all the latest-greatest concerts and sporting events. He enjoys reading, fishing, thrifting, bocci, painting, bowling, pickleball, time with his family, and dates with his wife.

Keep informed of special deals, giveaways, new releases, and exclusive updates from Creston: **CrestonMapes.com/contact**

For Creston's eBooks, audio books, and paperbacks: **Amazon.-com/author/crestonmapes**

STAND ALONE THRILLERS
Celebrity Pastor
I Am In Here
Nobody

SIGNS OF LIFE SERIES
Signs of Life
Let My Daughter Go
I Pick You
Charm Artist
Son & Shield
Secrets in Shadows

THE CRITTENDON FILES
Fear Has a Name
Poison Town
Sky Zone

ROCK STAR CHRONICLES
Dark Star: Confessions of a Rock Idol
Full Tilt

Made in the USA
Columbia, SC
05 September 2024

41797157R10117